"I LOATHE YOU JACK JACOBS. I DON'T KNOW HOW I ever got involved with you," Jill said.

His eyes darkened and a muscle jumped in his jaw. He drew her against his chest. "You've been waiting five years to say that. Feel better now? Or would you like to say it again?"

She curled her hands into fists on his chest. "Once will do, thanks. But I'd really feel better if I never had to see you again."

"I don't think that's what you want at all." His voice deepened, and he looked at her mouth for one heady moment. When he lifted his gaze to hers, she saw something strong and hot in his eyes. Anger. Awareness. The kind of intimacy that was never severed, even after the relationship that created it was.

He bent his head toward hers, his eyes dark with emotion. "Either hit me or kiss me, Jilly. That's what you want."

"Don't flatter yourself. You don't affect me that much one way or another."

He pulled her closer. "You're a poor liar, Jill Lansing."

"And you're insufferable—"

"Which is it going to be? Are you going to hit me or . . ." He lowered his eyes to her mouth again, and the feelings she'd been fighting took her by storm . . .

WHAT ARE *LOVESWEPT* ROMANCES?

They are stories of true romance and touching emotion. We believe those two very important ingredients are constants in our highly sensual and very believable stories in the LOVE-SWEPT line. Our goal is to give you, the reader, stories of consistently high quality that may sometimes make you laugh, sometimes make you cry, but are always fresh and creative and contain many delightful surprises within their pages.

Most romance fans read an enormous number of books. Those they truly love, they keep. Others may be traded with friends and soon forgotten. We hope that each LOVESWEPT romance will be a treasure—a "keeper." We will always try to publish

LOVE STORIES YOU'LL NEVER FORGET
BY AUTHORS YOU'LL ALWAYS REMEMBER

The Editors

Loveswept ®740

SLOW HEAT

ERICA SPINDLER

BANTAM BOOKS
NEW YORK · TORONTO · LONDON · SYDNEY · AUCKLAND

SLOW HEAT

A Bantam Book / May 1995

Loveswept
Bantam Books
P.O. Box 985
Hicksville, NY 11802

ISBN 0-553-44516-2

Published simultaneously in the United States and Canada

Bantam Books are published by Bantam Books, a division of Bantam Dou-
bleday Dell Publishing Group, Inc. Its trademark, consisting of the words
"Bantam Books" and the portrayal of a rooster, is Registered in U.S.
Patent and Trademark Office and in other countries. Marca Registrada.
Bantam Books, 1540 Broadway, New York, New York 10036.

PRINTED IN THE UNITED STATES OF AMERICA

OPM   10 9 8 7 6 5 4 3 2 1

ONE

Jill Lansing smiled to herself as she pulled into the KTBC-TV parking lot. She angled her Volvo into the first available spot and cut off the engine. She smiled again. Today was the day her idea for a movie-review show that responded to women's likes and dislikes would become a reality. She'd conceived the show several years before, during a heated discussion with a fellow reviewer on the male bias of the review system.

Reel Reviews. Her program. Her big chance.

It was almost too good to be true.

Jill flipped down her visor, made a quick inspection of her hair and lipstick in the mirror, then snapped it back into place. She stepped out of the car, and sunshine spilled over her. She lifted her face to the cloudless blue sky. Even the weather had cooperated. But then, in southern California it always did.

She crossed the parking lot and within moments stepped through the station's double glass doors and took the elevator up to the executive floor. "Morning,

Annie," she called to the receptionist, crossing to her desk. "Great blouse."

"Thanks. It's new, but don't tell my husband." Annie smiled. "You must be excited."

Laughing, Jill leaned conspiratorially toward the other woman. "I'm so excited, I could swear it was Christmas morning."

The receptionist laughed. "Dana's in her office, ready and waiting. Go on back. And good luck!"

Jill waved in thanks and headed down the corridor that led to Dana Hoban's office. Dana was the producer of *Reel Reviews* and a good friend. They'd met three years ago at a party of a mutual acquaintance. Both had been recently divorced, both raw and in need of a friend. The friendship they'd formed that night had lasted even after their wounds had healed.

Dana's office door stood ajar. Jill tapped on it, then stepped inside. Dana looked up from her desk and smiled. "You're here. Good."

Jill returned the smile. "You didn't think I'd be late today, did you?" She dropped her briefcase onto one of the two chairs that faced Dana's desk. "Where's Clayton?" She had expected her fellow reviewer to be as anxious to get started as she was. "Don't tell me he slept in?"

Dana's smile faded. "We've got a problem."

"A problem?" Jill repeated, drawing her eyebrows together in concern. "What's wrong?"

"It's Clayton." Dana stood and came around the desk. "He's been arrested."

"Arrested!" Jill made a sound of shocked disbelief. "What for?"

"Drugs."

"No." Jill brought a hand to her chest. "Surely there's some mistake. Drugs? Clayton? I can't imagine."

"There's no mistake. He was stopped for reckless driving, and the police discovered a gram of cocaine on the seat beside him." Dana shoved her hands into her blazer's front pockets. "This is his first offense, so he probably won't go to jail. But he will have to do time in a rehab center."

Jill still couldn't believe it, even though she knew it must be true. Clayton had always seemed so dependable and conservative. "When did this happen?"

"Thursday night. I tried to call you. In fact I tried all weekend. Where were you?"

"My parents were in San Francisco for the weekend, Rebecca was with her father, so I just . . . went." Jill studied her friend's serious expression, a sinking sensation in the pit of her stomach. "Does this mean . . . Is the show being shelved until we can find another reviewer?"

"We've already found one."

"You have?" Confused, Jill shook her head. "You replaced Clayton already? So quickly?" The producer nodded, and Jill took an involuntary step back, stunned. "But, Dana, how could you have made that decision without consulting—"

"Hello, Jill."

The man's voice moved over her like warm, weathered silk, calling so strongly to her memory that she caught her breath. *Jack Jacobs. It couldn't be.* She brought a hand to her mouth. *Not Jack.*

Even as she reassured herself that her ears and memory were playing a cruel trick on her, her heart began to thunder, her palms to sweat. She turned slowly, a prayer on the tip of her tongue.

Her prayer went unanswered.

Jack stood in the doorway, his dark head cocked, his lips curved into the wicked, amused half smile she remembered from when they'd been together. She hadn't seen him in five years, not since the morning she'd realized the hopelessness of their relationship and walked out of his life. She moved her gaze over him, looking for changes, finding few. He still dressed with a rough panache, his body appearing as hard and lean as it had been back then. The lines of his face were more deeply etched than before, but it only made him more handsome, more appealing. There had always been something unique about Jack's face, about the way he carried himself, something bold, lawless even.

She returned her gaze to his face, and their eyes met. For one electric moment she was twenty-five again and looking into her lover's deep-blue eyes. She felt the pull, the buzz of sexual awareness move through her.

She shook off the sensation, unnerved that even after all the time that had passed, just looking at Jack could affect her so strongly. "Jack," she managed, her voice thick.

"You two know each other?" Dana said, obviously surprised.

"We did," Jack said quietly. "A long time ago."

"No kidding? This is a small worl—"

"Dana, excuse me." Her assistant popped her head around the door. "Daniel wants to see you in his office. Immediately."

"Thanks." Dana checked her watch. "You kids get reacquainted. I'll be back in a minute."

Jill watched Dana rush out of the office, wishing she could go with her, wishing she could be anywhere but here, doing anything but facing the man who had hurt her so badly that she had thought she would never be whole again.

She turned back to him and found him studying her, his expression serious. "Nothing to say, Jilly?" he said finally, softly.

Jilly. It had been his pet name for her. When they'd been lovers. His use of it made her feel exposed, vulnerable. She swallowed hard. "How have you been?"

One corner of his mouth lifted in a crooked smile. "Great. And you?"

"Good." She cleared her throat. "How are things at *People?*"

"Great. How do you like the *L.A. Times?*"

"I love it."

He slipped his fingers into the front pockets of his light-colored denims and moved his gaze over her, as if taking in every detail. "You look wonderful," he murmured, bringing his eyes back to hers. "You haven't changed."

Hadn't she? She felt worlds different from the twenty-five-year-old girl she'd been then. But still, at his comment a flutter of pleasure washed over her. She shouldn't care what he thought of her appearance, she shouldn't be so gratified that he thought she looked good. But she was. The truth of that took her breath away.

She laced her fingers. "Thank you."

He dropped his gaze to her mouth, letting it linger there for one heady moment, then lifted it back to hers. "I hear you have a child."

Her beautiful Becky. She drew in a silent, calming breath. "Yes. Rebecca will be five in March."

"Five?" he repeated, almost to himself. "She could have been ours."

Jill sucked in a sharp breath, his words twisting inside her like a blade. "You didn't want a family, remember? You didn't want me."

"I always wanted you, Jill."

"But you didn't want me for always. You couldn't promise me more than the moment." She searched his face. "Did you expect me to wait forever?" she asked, her voice shaking. "Is that what you wanted?"

His mouth twisted, and he closed the distance between them, stopping so close, she felt the heat of his body, caught the faint scent of the spicy soap he always used. She squeezed her eyes shut, remembering the way it had been between them. Aching for him to touch her. Praying that he wouldn't.

"I don't know what I expected," he said tightly. "But I know what I didn't expect, to come home to a Dear John letter."

She felt his words like a stunning blow. "Would you have rather we'd faced each other one more time? I thought there'd been too many scenes between us already. Would one more have changed anything?"

He muttered an oath and crossed to the window and gazed out at the Los Angeles skyline. For long moments he said nothing, then he looked over his shoulder at her. "Maybe. But we'll never know, will we?"

Something in his tone, in the expression in his eyes, tugged at her. Something akin to regret. Jack had changed, she realized. Something—or someone—had changed him.

She shook her head and called herself a fool. It didn't matter if or how Jack Jacobs had changed. He hadn't been able to make a commitment to her, even a vague one, so she'd left. She'd had to protect herself, her heart. Their relationship had ended a long time ago.

"If you were any kind of a gentleman, you'd bow out of the show now."

He laughed and leaned against the edge of the desk. "But I'm no gentleman. You know that. Besides, I've already signed on the dotted line." He arched his eyebrows, the picture of the man she remembered from five years ago—cocky, confident, daunted by no one nor by anything. "Afraid I'll show you up?"

"Only in your dreams, Jacobs." She crossed to him and looked him straight in the eye. "You're an overconfident, boorish, chauvinist jerk. I think your reviews are outrageously biased, and I'd rather work with a snake."

He lifted his lips in a lazy, amused smile. "Running scared already. I like that."

Her blood pressure skyrocketed. She didn't know why she should be surprised by that. He'd always had this effect on her, had always been able to break through her reserve and make her mad as hell. "You self-absorbed, irreverent son-of-a—"

"Sorry about that." Dana breezed back into the room, stopping suddenly, looking from one of them to the other. "Is something wrong?"

Jill swung to face her friend. "I'm at a bit of a disadvantage here, Dana. Could we speak privately?"

The producer nodded, then turned to Jack. "There's a break room down the hall to the right. Do you mind?"

"Not at all."

Jill watched him stride from the room, her chest

tight. She knew in her gut that there was nothing she would be able to do about working with Jack; she was stuck with him. But she had to try anyway.

She met her friend's concerned gaze. "How could you do this without consulting me, Dana? We conceived this show together. Couldn't the decision have waited a couple of days until you could reach me?"

"There wasn't time." Dana tipped her hands palms up. "We go into production today, we had to move fast. In truth we were damn lucky to get Jack on such short notice."

The producer took a step toward her, her expression sympathetic. "Look, I understand the way you feel, and I'm sorry. But the station has a lot at stake with this program, Jill. So do I. And the fact of the matter is, I'm not the sole decision maker around here. And the powers that be, including me, thought Jack was the best choice. We thought you and Jack would make perfect partners."

Perfect partners. Jill sucked in a sharp breath. How those words mocked her. Five years ago she had thought the same about the two of them. She had been proved a naive fool.

"How could you think him the best choice? The man's a Neanderthal."

Dana laughed and shook her head, her short dark hair fluttering around her face. "Neanderthals are good for ratings. The female viewers are going to love him." Jill scowled and Dana laughed again. "You have to admit, movie reviewers don't usually look like leading men themselves. Jack Jacobs does."

Jill couldn't argue with that. She tried another tack.

"But we're so different. Our review styles. Our approach to evaluating films. Our backgrounds."

"Which is exactly why we chose him." Dana's dark eyes gleamed with excitement. "Out of a hundred films, you and Jack only agreed wholeheartedly on a dozen of them. Twelve, Jill! That's just over ten percent."

"Only because he's always wrong. The man has no taste."

A grin tugged at the producer's mouth. "Funny, he said the same thing about you."

Jill took another stab. "But don't you think the viewers will be confused by the dichotomy of our reviews? Don't you think—"

"No. I think they're going to love it."

Jill turned away from her friend and crossed to the window. Below, the traffic had become even more snarled. Hopelessly so, Jill thought.

She had to tell Dana everything. Because of the show. And because they were friends.

"Jill?"

She dragged her gaze from the gridlock below to look at the other woman. Jill smiled sadly. "There's something you don't know about me, about a part of my life. Something I never told you."

"So tell me now."

Jill hesitated, then took a deep breath. "Jack and I were lovers," she murmured. "Years before you and I met. It ended badly. Very badly. At least for me."

"I'm sorry," Dana said quietly. "I wish I'd known."

"There never seemed a reason to dredge up that particular piece of my past." She shrugged and looked out at the brilliant day once more. "Until today I considered it ancient history."

"How ancient, Jill? What do you feel for him?"

"Besides total disdain?" Jill laughed, the sound fragile, edgy. "He hurt me badly. But I've had five years to recover." She met her friend's eyes. "I'm over him, Dana."

The producer slipped her hands into her blazer pockets and cocked her head. "He's under contract, Jill. And so are you. You guys have to work together. Tell me that's not going to present a problem."

"What if I couldn't tell you that?"

Dana pursed her lips. "I don't know, Jill. I just don't know what would happen."

Somebody on the team was committed to Jack being one of the reviewers, Jill realized. Somebody with clout. If she made trouble, it could be herself who was out of the job, not Jack.

That wasn't going to happen. She wouldn't be the one who made trouble.

Jill squared her shoulders. "All the other review shows are hosted by men. By far the great majority of reviewers are men, with men holding the majority of the positions with the big papers and periodicals. We put this show together as a way for a female reviewer's voice to be heard. I'm committed to making this show work. You know that, Dana."

"Yes, I do. But you know, nothing you just said answers my question."

Jill took a deep breath. "I'm a professional, Dana. I can keep my personal feelings from interfering with the job I have to do."

"Thank God." Dana put her hand to her heart. "You gave me a scare, Jill. I want this show to be a success. I'm banking on it."

"No more than I am." Jill laughed, her tension easing, her self-confidence returning. "Actually I'm starting to like the idea of going head-to-head with Jack."

"Hoping you'll bloody his?" Dana asked dryly.

"You really want me to answer that?" Jill smiled sweetly.

Dana made a face. "Maybe not. Did I tell you we're thinking of changing the title of the show? You know, incorporate your names somehow. Jack and Jill something . . . it's too great a coincidence not to cash in on it."

At Jill's groan the producer laughed. "Just a joke, but you have to admit it's cute. It's catchy. People like that."

Jill grinned. "Sure, but people like junk food and paintings on black velvet too."

Dana laughed again. "Sue me, but I have this feeling that the viewers are going to tune in as much for the fireworks as the reviews."

"If it's fireworks you want . . ." Jill let the question trail off suggestively, and Dana wrinkled her nose and started for the door.

"Maybe I'd better amend that. Come on, let's go get your Neanderthal and a cup of coffee. It's going to be a long morning."

Jack watched Jill hurry across the KTBC parking lot. Sunshine shot her light-brown hair with gold, drenching her in light. She didn't look back, didn't hesitate. But then, she hadn't said good-bye either. Standard operating procedure for Jill Lansing.

A dozen different emotions barreled over him, and Jack narrowed his eyes, attempting to shake them off.

She'd barely acknowledged his presence during their meeting with Dana, refusing to speak directly to him or meet his eyes.

But he hadn't been able to keep his eyes off of her. Physically she'd changed little in the five years since he'd seen her last. A shorter hairstyle. A new perfume. New shade of lipstick.

Looking at her still did something to him. Stirred his blood. Moved his senses in a way no other woman ever had. Jack started for his car. Living in southern California, an area celebrated for its beautiful women, Jill had always stood out even though she was neither traditionally nor exotically beautiful. She possessed a natural, wholesome kind of beauty; she radiated warmth and intelligence. Her brown gaze was always straightforward, her smile sincere.

But in other ways she'd changed drastically. She was a mother now, after all. She'd been married and divorced. He sucked in a quick, sharp breath. The Jill he'd known had been softer, more open. She'd worn her emotions on her sleeve and been the kind of person who could make even a hardened cynic believe in happily-ever-after.

A sense of loss moved over him, surprising him with its intensity. He shook it off and called himself a fool. His relationship with Jill had ended a long time ago. He'd just barely averted disaster. She'd wanted a husband, had wanted children. She'd never wanted him, not really.

She'd proved that. Within six months of walking out on their relationship, she'd been married to somebody else.

She'd gotten what she wanted. She always did.

He flexed his fingers in frustration. Then why had he looked at her and ached? Why had he been flooded with memories? Seeing her should have been a piece of cake. He'd grown up. A lot of time had passed. He'd told himself he would enjoy working with her; he'd told himself they were simply two professionals who happened to have a past together.

Instead he'd looked at her and remembered everything. The way she'd felt in his arms, his bed. The way she'd filled his days and hours with light and warmth and . . . contentment. The way those things had made him feel confined.

And he'd remembered their last fight, when she'd told him she was pregnant, remembered the verbal bullets they had shot at each other, remembered the way he had felt as he'd rushed to catch his flight to Cannes—ripped wide and bleeding, terrified and trapped. He'd often wondered if she'd felt the same way. But then, he couldn't be sure she had felt anything at all.

After that there'd been nothing else to remember—he'd returned from his assignment to find her gone. Their apartment had been stripped of every evidence of her. Except for the note. *False alarm*, the note had read. *I'm not pregnant, after all. Congratulations.*

There'd been no baby. The home pregnancy test had been wrong.

He'd stared at the note, the words blurring before his eyes, emotion churning inside him. He hadn't known what to think or do; it had felt as if the rug had been pulled out from under his life.

And now she acted like she was the only one who had

been hurt. She acted like she was the only one who'd had a stake in their relationship.

Muttering another oath, Jack unlocked his car and slipped inside. Curving his fingers around the steering wheel, he rested his head against the seat back. He'd always been honest with her. Always. The night they'd first met, when it had become clear that they weren't going to be able to deny the sparks between them, he'd told her that marriage was not in his plans, had told her he never wanted a family. Never.

He hadn't wanted her to have any illusions about him. He hadn't wanted her to hate him someday for not giving her an out, or to accuse him of being dishonest.

But she hadn't believed him. She'd thought she could change his mind—and when she hadn't been able to, she'd blown him off.

And had gotten what she wanted with somebody else. A baby. A little girl named Rebecca.

He tightened his fingers on the wheel until they went numb. He breathed deeply, willing away the rush of emotion that swept over him. As he had hundreds of times in the last five years, he reminded himself that fatherhood wasn't for him. He reminded himself of his vows to avoid it and marriage at all costs, that avoiding them was a matter of survival.

But he'd never forgotten the way he'd felt, even if only for those few days at Cannes, thinking that a part of him was growing inside Jill.

He swore again and started his car. Jill had turned him inside out and backward, then just walked out. She'd used him.

Up ahead he saw her cautiously maneuver her Volvo

into traffic. He watched until the white car disappeared from sight, then whipped his own car out of its parking spot, burning rubber as he did.

She wouldn't use him again. And he'd be damned if he would let her turn him inside out and backward. This time, he vowed, Jill Lansing would have no effect on him at all.

TWO

Right on time. Jill clasped her hands in front of her and watched her ex-husband drive slowly through the front gate, excitement and expectation trembling inside her. Becky was home. In a matter of moments she would be with her little girl again.

He stopped the car, and the front passenger door flew open. Rebecca burst out of it and raced toward her, her face wreathed in a brilliant smile.

"Mommy!"

"Rebecca!" Laughing, Jill squatted down and held out her arms. In seconds the little girl had launched herself into them and was hugging her tightly.

"Hi, baby," Jill said, hugging her back, squeezing her tightly. "I missed you so much."

"Missed you, too, Mommy."

Jill smiled and pressed a kiss on the top of her daughter's head. Rebecca made a sound of contentment and snuggled closer into her mother's arms. Her little-girl scent filled Jill's head, and Jill breathed deeply. The two weeks since she'd seen her daughter had seemed like an eternity. She wouldn't think about the fact that two weeks from now she would be without her again.

Her ex-husband climbed out of the car and started toward them, bringing Becky's overnight bags. He set them down on the sidewalk beside them and slipped his hands into his front trouser pockets. "Hello, Jill."

Jill lifted her gaze to his face. His tight expression belied his casual stance and tone. "Peter." She scooped Rebecca into her arms and stood. "How did it go?"

"Great. As always."

Jill stroked Becky's silky brown hair—hair the exact shade of her own. "No nightmares or sniffles or anything else I should know about?"

"Not a thing."

"Good." She took a deep breath. "How's the baby?"

"Getting bigger every day. She—"

"She's so cute, Mommy! You should see." Rebecca tipped her head back to meet her mother's gaze. "She smiled at me. I gave her my Raggedy to play with an' she smiled at me."

Peter beamed at his daughter. "She smiled because she loves her big sister."

Rebecca straightened, practically oozing sisterly pride. "I'm a good big sissy."

Jill's chest tightened. It hurt to see Rebecca's affection for her half sister, hurt because Peter was able to give Rebecca what she could not—a traditional family and home life. The kind she had always yearned for. That she still yearned for.

She cleared her throat. "Becky, baby, give your daddy a hug and a kiss. We need to go in."

She handed Rebecca over and watched her hug and kiss Peter. Moments like these were so painful, they took her breath. Not because she still loved Peter, but because her daughter loved him so much. Rebecca deserved to have a mother and father who lived together. She deserved to have a traditional family, one who shared evening meals and holidays. A family who attended church on Sundays and took vacations in July.

Instead she was shuttled between her two parents. Instead she had two homes, two sets of toys and friends, two neighborhoods. She had a stepmother and a half sister, and parents who exchanged civil conversation when they came face-to-face while dropping her off or picking her up.

"Oh, look!" Becky squealed, pointing. "Kitty!"

The little girl squirmed and Peter let her down, and they watched as their daughter raced into the courtyard after the neighbor's big tabby cat named Butch.

Jill smiled. "She loves animals so much."

"That's why Jeanne and I got her a kitten." Peter shifted his gaze to Jill. "She named him Kitty Kitty. She hated to leave him."

The superiority and accusation in his tone set Jill's teeth on edge. She met his eyes. Peter had left her; he had been the one who had filed for divorce. Yet he blamed her for their breakup. He'd accused her of not loving him enough. She'd been a faithful, devoted wife, a loving mother. She would have stayed with him forever, just as she'd promised in her wedding vows.

Yet he still blamed her.

She thought of Jack; his image filled her head and senses. Guilt barreled over her, and she shook it off. She had married Peter in good faith; she had devoted herself to making the marriage work. She had done nothing to feel guilty about.

She looked him straight in the eye. "Perhaps, considering the circumstances, getting her a pet wasn't such a good idea. Besides, I thought we'd decided she wasn't old enough for a pet."

"You decided," he snapped. "And the circumstances will be changing soon."

"Not that soon. Kindergarten is still almost a year off." Jill took a step back. "I'm sure you need to get on your way. You have a long drive."

He caught her arm. "We need to talk about this."

She shook her head. "I don't think so. Like I said, we have plenty of time. Besides, Becky's right here."

"She's across the courtyard playing with the cat. She can't hear us." He lowered his voice. "This problem isn't going to go away, Jill. When Becky starts kindergarten, our joint-custody arrangement isn't going to work anymore. If we get this taken care of now, she'll be adjusted to her new living situation before school starts." He looked away, then back, his gaze determined. "I want her to live with me."

She'd expected this; it wasn't a surprise. The blood pounded in her head anyway. She took a deep, steadying breath. "And I want her with me. I'm her mother."

"And I'm her father."

Jill squeezed her fingers into fists, anger at his arrogant tone surging through her. "You're a good father, Peter, and I know you love her. She loves you too. I'm glad she has you, but she belongs with me."

He narrowed his eyes. "I disagree. And so does Jeanne."

"Jeanne has no say in this! *We're* her parents." The words spilled out, high and angry. She pressed a hand to her chest. "I'm her mother. I should be raising her, not

Jeanne. And if you got permanent custody, Jeanne would be raising her, not you. Be honest, we both know how hectic your work schedule is."

"What about your work schedule? At least Jeanne is home all day."

"My work is flexible. If Rebecca needs me, I'm available. Can you say the same?"

"It's obvious that we're never going to agree about this. That's why we need a judge." Peter squared his shoulders. "I haven't a doubt that he'll see the kind of stable family life I can give Becky and grant me custody."

His words cut her so deeply, so close to the heart of her wishes and fears, they took her breath. Just as he had known they would. "Why are you doing this to me?" she asked softly, narrowing her eyes. "Is this about making me pay? Is it about hurting me?"

"What if part of it is, Jill?"

"The divorce was your idea, Peter. Not mine. And Rebecca is the one who's going to be hurt most by this."

"I disagree." He lifted his shoulders. "Besides, none of my other motivations change the fact that I love my daughter and want her with me full-time."

"Mommy . . . Daddy! Look! Butterfly!"

She and Peter both turned to their daughter and exclaimed over the butterfly. Moments later her ex-husband drove away. But their exchange ate at Jill for the rest of the night, dimming the pleasure of being with her daughter again, the pleasure of their nighttime rituals.

Long after Rebecca had fallen asleep, Jill continued to sit on the edge of her bed, stroking her hair and humming a lullaby. She loved Rebecca so much that at times she thought she might burst with the emotion. Rebecca was everything sweet and good about her life; she couldn't bear to lose her. She didn't know how she could go on if Peter got custody.

Fear rose inside her, and she forced it back. No. It wasn't going to happen. What judge would award custody to a father when the mother was good and fit? She wasn't about to let Peter's threat steal the beauty of this moment. She would contact a lawyer, file for full custody, and everything would be fine.

Bending, Jill brushed her mouth against Rebecca's warm, velvety cheek. "Sweet dreams, baby," she whispered, smiling softly. "See you in the morning."

The hum of activity filled the studio. The floor manager called last-minute directions to the audio engineer; stagehands stood on ladders, awaiting the lighting director's final instructions; and Dana, their director, Tim, and the camera crew seemed to be everywhere at once.

Jill watched the frenetic goings-on from the side of the set, her palms damp, her stomach aflutter. She hadn't been calm, not really, since her talk with Peter. Calling the lawyer a friend had recommended hadn't helped. He'd told her not to take her husband's desire for full custody lightly—more and more judges were awarding custody to fathers. But he'd also told her not to worry unduly and had arranged an appointment for her to come talk to him about the situation.

Jill pressed the flat of her hand to her fluttering stomach. But her present butterflies, she knew, had to do with the show. She was nervous about sitting in front of the camera, anxious about her appearance, her performance, the viewers' response to her.

She took a deep, calming breath. She had nothing to worry about. She'd done television before; she'd reviewed the movies for today's show and had spent a great deal of time preparing what she would say about each one. Her reviews had been inputted onto the Tele-Prompter along with the director's instructions, and earlier today she and Jack had met with the staff and crew and had gone over every detail of the show, from the lighting to the audio to the placement of the commercial breaks.

She knew what to expect, when to expect it and was confident she could pull it off.

Jack.

Jill sucked in a quick breath, acknowledging the truth. Her nerves had little to do with the show itself, but everything to do with working beside Jack. He had the ability to stir her emotions without trying, had the ability to make her forget about being serious and professional and in control. With Jack she simply reacted.

She caught sight of him winding his way through the mix of people, deep in conversation with the assistant producer. They stopped directly across the set from her, and she moved her gaze almost greedily over him. No stodgy dress shirt and tie for Jack. He wore a loose-fitting jacket, a navy T-shirt underneath, and light-colored denims.

And he looked wonderful. She wished she could think otherwise, wished she could look at him and not feel a stirring of admiration and awareness, but no matter how much she wanted to, she couldn't. The blasted man practically oozed sex appeal.

Jill drew her eyebrows together. Dana and the other powers-that-be had decided on a younger, hipper look for her and Jack and the show, a cross between an MTV veejay and a traditional talk-show host.

Actually Jack had played a major part in that decision. He'd argued that *Reel Reviews* needed a different look from the other review shows, whose hosts looked like nerdy college professors. He'd reminded them that this was, after all, the entertainment industry, and Los Angeles the entertainment capital of the world.

So here she was, a thirty-year-old mother and professional woman, wearing a ridiculously small bit of spandex. Jill frowned and tugged at the hem of the navy-blue minidress. If not for the oversized mesh shawl draped diagonally across her right shoulder, she would feel completely exposed.

She looked at Jack again, taking in his comfortable garb. This was his fault, and she would like to wring his neck.

As if he read her thoughts, Jack looked up and met her eyes. For one endless moment he gazed at her, then his lips curved into a cocky, confident smile.

The butterflies in her stomach burst into flight.

Lifting his hand in a mock salute, he turned and walked away. She muttered an oath and curved her fingers into fists. Blast the man! And blast her own inability to ignore him. Working alongside him the past two days had been a challenge. She'd been determined that he not affect her, had been determined that she wouldn't remember or dwell on the past.

She'd failed miserably. For as hard as she'd tried, as determined as she'd been, she looked at him and remembered everything—the good and the bad, the perfect and the perfectly painful. She looked at him and remembered Peter's accusations and the part Jack had unwittingly played in her present situation.

What did he see when he looked at her? she wondered. What did he remember?

She swore silently. It didn't matter. She and Jack would work together to make *Reel Reviews* a success; there their involvement with each other stopped.

Straightening her shoulders with determination, she turned her attention to the set she and Jack would occupy minutes from now. To the at-home viewers, it would appear that she and Jack were sitting in a movie theater and that the movie clips were being shown on a screen. Their seats resembled standard theater seats, though they were larger, spaced farther apart and swiveled so that she and Jack could face each other.

Almost show time. Almost time to face Jack.

As if her thoughts had conjured him, he appeared beside her. She didn't look at him; she didn't have to. She would have known it was he if she'd been deaf and blind. His presence charged the air; she felt his heat, his energy. And she smelled him, his spicy soap, the scent of his shampoo, his skin.

"Great dress," he said after a moment, amusement coloring his tone.

His deep voice moved over her like warm, weathered silk. She steeled herself against the sensation. And against the flutter of feminine pleasure at the appreciation she saw in his eyes. "Is that what they're calling four inches of elastic these days? Interesting," she commented.

"I'd say so." He lowered his voice. "Extremely interesting."

Heat eased up her cheeks, and she turned and glared

at him. The man could charm white off of rice. "Can it, Jacobs. This dress is your fault, and when I get a chance, I'm going to pay you back big-time."

He tipped his head back and laughed. "Hey, don't look at me. I didn't pick out that . . . dress."

An involuntary smile tugged at her mouth. She placed her fists on her hips. "If it wasn't for your bright idea, I'd be wearing a sensible skirt and blazer right now."

"And looking like a spinster librarian."

"Better than an oversexed bubble head."

"That's a matter of opinion." At her look he held up his hands, laughing. "If it will make you feel any better, you don't look like a bubble head. You couldn't, even if your life depended on it. Now, oversexed . . . that's another matter."

The flutter of pleasure, of awareness, returned. She made a sound of irritation. How could he get to her so easily? So effortlessly? "You are the most annoying man I have ever known."

"I guess that means you're not going to give me a clue what you thought about this week's movies?"

"What? And ruin the surprise?"

"I don't like surprises. Remember?"

She batted her eyelashes in exaggerated innocence. "Oh, that's right. But surprises are what Dana and Tim want. Maybe you should spare yourself all that misery and resign from the show."

One corner of his mouth lifted. "Fat chance. But nice try anyway."

"I do my best." She smiled sweetly.

"Mmm." He shifted his gaze to the set. "Looks like they're about ready for us. Nervous?"

"A bit. Are you?"

"A bit."

His lips curved up in amusement, and she cocked her head. The Jack she'd known had been afraid of no one and nothing. He'd approached every challenge, every new hurdle, as if it were a country to be conquered. It was the way he'd approached life, the way he'd approached her.

Only this time she wouldn't be conquered.

"You're not nervous at all," she murmured. "You enjoy adrenaline. You enjoy a bit of danger. I think the closer to the edge you are, the more exciting you find it."

He moved his gaze slowly over her before meeting her eyes once more. "Then you must have been the highest, the most deadly of all precipices."

Jill caught her breath; her pulse began to thud. "I know what you're doing, Jack. And it won't work, so stop it."

"Stop what, Jill? What am I doing?" He touched her cheek with his fingertip, so lightly, she could have imagined it—if not for the way the blood rushed to her head, if not for the flood of heat that left her weak-kneed and aching.

She jerked her head away. "You're trying to unnerve me. Trying to blow my concentration."

"And why would I do that?" he asked softly. "We're a team here."

A team. Memories flooded her, hurt and longings with them. She shook her head. "I don't think so. You've never been a team player, Jack. As I recall, you prided yourself on standing alone. On being a free agent, a loner."

"People change."

"Not that much."

He gazed at her, something in his eyes tugging at her. Something bleak. Something that hurt. Then he shot her a wicked smile. "Don't worry, Jilly. I'll go easy on you."

"Easy on me?" she repeated, incredulous.

"Sure," he drawled, lifting his shoulders. "After all, you are the younger, less experienced member of the team."

"Is that so?" She arched her eyebrows at the challenge. "Underestimate me and you'll have a problem, because I plan to be relentless."

"Sounds like you want this to be war." He leaned toward her. "Better be sure that's what you want, Jilly. Because I'll play to win."

"And so will I." She met his gaze evenly. "With us I don't think there's any other way. Not anymore."

He opened his mouth to respond, then closed it as Dana hurried over, all smiles. "You kids ready?"

"As ready as we'll ever be." Jack met Jill's eyes. "Right, partner?"

She inched up her chin. "Right."

"I'll be in the control booth during taping," Dana said as they started for the set. "If there's a problem, Tim will be on the floor. He and I will be communicating by headphones."

The producer let out a pent-up breath, obviously running on adrenaline. "Don't worry if you stumble over your words or make a mistake. That's the beauty of taping; if we need to, we can do it over." She motioned them to their seats. "Once you take your places, the lighting director will make her final adjustments and we'll get started. Any questions?"

Neither she nor Jack had any, and before Jill had a chance to think about how nervous she was, they were through the show's introductions and watching the first clip.

Heart thundering, palms damp, Jill watched the clip. *A Choice for Love.* She'd liked this movie. In fact she'd loved it. The story of a retarded boy, his single mother, and the man who comes into their lives and changes them forever, had touched her, had tugged shamelessly at her heartstrings.

The clip ended and, as directed, she looked at camera number one. "Director Evan Fieldman has created a touching story about the challenges of loving a special child, and how those bonds can be strained when a stranger becomes involved with the family.

"Newcomer Brian James is outstanding as little Stevie, and as always Meryl Streep is incomparable as his mother, a woman torn by two very different, but equally pressing needs."

Jill took an easy breath, wondering why she'd been so nervous. "I was impressed with Pete Rawlings's script. He managed to make something fresh out of the age-old triangle—woman and child, woman and lover. Thrown into the scenario is a concerned father, admirably played by Ben Kingsley, and a wacky next-door neighbor played to perfection by Mercedes Ruehl."

She turned to face Jack. "I have to say, *A Choice for Love* is one of the best movies I've seen this year. Full of heart and hope and realism."

Something passed across Jack's expression, lightning

quick, but in that instant she knew the first shot in their war had been fired.

"Gee, Jill, what can I say? We're going to disagree right off the bat." Jack flashed her one of his infuriatingly sexy smiles, then swung his gaze to the camera. "I thought the story was not only contrived, but full of cornball sentiment. I don't think a writer could hit any more false notes than Rawlings did here. This doesn't hold a candle to his earlier work—*Judging the Joneses* and *Out of Time.*"

He lifted his hands, palms up. "Meryl Streep did the best she could with the material, but the boy who played Stevie was positively wooden. And Kingsley and Ruehl were wasted here." He met her eyes again. "I think you're way off the mark with this one, Jill."

She leaned forward in her seat, incredulous. "You can't tell me the scene when the mother is forced to choose a care facility for her son didn't strike a chord of absolute realism in you? You didn't feel the pain she was going through, you didn't share in the agony of having to face such a difficult, no-win situation?"

"That's exactly what I'm saying. It all seemed so soap-opera, so . . . well, overwrought. I never forgot for a moment that I was watching a movie. And not a very skillfully crafted one at that."

She shook her head in outraged disbelief. At his words and at his condescending tone. "If this movie didn't tug at your heartstrings, then perhaps you have none, Jack."

"Perhaps. Or could it be that your own taste runs a bit to the overly sentimental side?" He lifted his shoulders. "But maybe it's just a woman's thing."

She bristled. *"Overly sentimental"? "A woman's*

thing"? The Neanderthal, chauvinist beast. "It doesn't matter whether a movie deals with male issues or female issues, good's good."

"Exactly. And in my opinion this missed the mark."

"And in mine it was right on."

Jack swung toward the camera once again, smiling disarmingly. "Up next, Sylvester Stallone in his best outing since the original *Rocky.*"

They made it through the entire show with a minimum of second takes. She'd hated the Stallone picture, had called it testosterone-laden junk; he'd thought it pure edge-of-your seat entertainment. They'd agreed about a third film, a cliché-laden comedy, but for dramatically different reasons. They'd grudgingly agreed on the merits of one film, a noncommercial piece about L.A. street gangs.

Jill closed her dressing-room door behind her and leaned against it, trembling so badly, she thought her legs might give. The taping had gone nothing as she had imagined or planned. She had imagined a lively but serious exchange of views and opinions. She had planned on presenting a warm but stoic demeanor.

Stoic? she thought, bringing her hands to her flushed cheeks. One small, knowing smile from Jack had turned her into a mouthy firebrand. She'd all but called Jack a chauvinist jerk; she had asked exactly where he'd gotten his training. Her heart had been racing, her adrenaline pumping. She had felt totally in control, yet at the same time completely out of control.

Sparring with Jack had been exciting. Exhilarating. She squeezed her eyes shut, her heart pounding against the wall of her chest. While slinging retorts at him, she'd felt alive. Vital and energized. But then, being around

Jack had always been a challenge, had always been exciting. Physically and intellectually.

Jill spun away from the door and crossed to the mirror. She gazed at her reflection, barely recognizing the flushed, bright-eyed woman gazing back at her. Being with Jack had been fun. Today and five years ago. When they'd been lovers, he had made her laugh, had made her carefree and daring; when with him she had forgotten about the importance of being in control and serious, she had forgotten that she had no one to rely on but herself.

She shook her head. It hadn't always been fun, she reminded herself. It hadn't been fun when they'd been hurting each other. And at the end there had been far more tears than laughs.

"Jill," Dana called, rapping softly on the door. "Are you decent?"

"Come on in, Dana," she called, turning nervously to face the door. The other woman had, no doubt, been just as surprised as Jill at the show's sudden change in direction, at the sudden change in Jill. What had Dana thought of it?

The producer entered the room, closing the door softly behind her. She met Jill's eyes, her expression unsettling.

The time of reckoning had come. Jill took a deep breath. "I know you're surprised, Dana. I am too. And I feel like a jerk for letting him get to me. But the things he said about that wonderful movie . . ." She shook her head. "I tried to bite my tongue, I tried to keep my professional cool and stick to the format we had discussed, but I just . . . couldn't. He rang all my bells."

Jill took another deep breath. "Although it was unplanned, I feel like it worked. It just seemed to click. But if you're unhappy, I'm sure we—"

"Unhappy?" Dana interrupted, laughing and moving farther into the room. "You guys were great." She closed the distance between them, clasping Jill's hands in her own. "Wonderful in fact."

"Wonderful?" Jill gazed at the other woman, relieved, pleased. "You thought we were great?"

The producer laughed again. "And so did everyone else. I think we've got a hit on our hands."

Jill smiled, then laughed, the sound giddy to her own ears. "A hit," she repeated breathlessly. "It's not too soon to tell?"

"A producer knows these things." Dana hugged her. "The chemistry between you and Jack was incredible. The set practically crackled with it. You two are a producer's dream. Wait until you see the tape—your eyes were sparkling, your cheeks were flushed. You looked like you wanted either to kiss him or kill him."

Jill groaned, embarrassed, and Dana grinned. "I've got to hand it to Jack. He's one hell of a showman. The way he ad-libbed his reactions to your comments was nothing short of incredible. He's got a real gift for timing. He could have been an actor, he's so good."

"What do you mean ad-libbed?" Jill drew her eyebrows together. "He didn't read off the TelePrompTer?"

"No. He reacted to you."

Jack hadn't read his reviews. He'd ad-libbed. Jill frowned again, not liking the thought running through her head.

Dana searched Jill's expression. "Did I say something wrong?"

"Of course not." Jill worked to keep her expression

and tone neutral. "I'm surprised, that's all. I'm glad you're pleased with the show."

"I really am." Dana crossed to the door, stopping and turning back to Jill. "By the way, you were right about the dress. It really wasn't you. We're going to go with something a bit more conservative next week."

"Thank God."

Dana smiled. "Plus, we want to play up the differences between you and Jack. You know, make him look hip and you look . . ."

Dana's words faltered, and Jill arched her eyebrows. "Was 'prim' the description you were looking for? 'Goody two-shoes'? Or even 'stodgy'?"

Dana cleared her throat. "No, we want a sweeter look. Something more . . . romantic."

"Romantic?"

"You know, more . . . feminine."

"More feminine!"

"Flowing skirts, lace collars. Things like that. Jack's a man, you're a woman; your reviews are going to reflect your differences."

"So, apparently, are our clothes." Jill made a sound of disgust. "I thought the whole purpose of this show was to give a large audience of women a female perspective on movies. I feel like I'm participating in a fashion show instead. I can't believe it could make such a difference what I wear."

"Ironic, isn't it? But if altering your look enhances the show's appeal, that many more women will hear your reviews." Dana grasped the doorknob and twisted it. "Go ahead and finish getting changed, we can talk later."

After the door shut behind Dana, Jill crossed to the

mirror and sat down. She gazed at her reflection a moment, her head whirling with everything that had happened in the past few hours. Jill smiled and began removing her makeup. Dana thought the show was going to be a hit. She thought she and Jack had been wonderful.

"Jack's one hell of a showman. He could have been an actor, he's so good."

A showman. An actor. Jill's smile faded. How much had Jack altered his reviews for effect? Surely he couldn't be so low as to have changed them much.

Or could he? Her frown deepened. When he wanted something badly, Jack was capable of anything.

And he wanted to put his mark on *Reel Reviews*.

Picking up her brush, she began to work the spray out of her hair. A week ago she'd had a firm grip on the show's direction. Everything had been under control, including her emotions. Jack had signed on and—wham! Everything had spun slightly out of her reach. Even what she wore was beyond her grasp.

She paused, the brush held in midstroke. Jack had been in complete control every moment. He'd had his plan for the show from the beginning, had known how to get a rise out of her and had gone for it.

She had played right into his hands.

Her mouth tightened and she dropped the brush to the vanity. She didn't like what she was thinking; she hoped it wasn't true. But she had to find out.

She changed quickly into her herringbone trousers and crisp white blouse, then slipped into her shoes. Without pausing for second thoughts, she marched out of her dressing room and across the hall to his.

Jill rapped on his door; a moment later he swung it

open. She felt her heart skip a beat. He wore a pair of form-hugging jeans—and nothing else. Partially unfastened, they hung low on his hips, revealing an intoxicating glimpse of his abdomen.

She moved her gaze unwittingly across his bare chest, and lower. Her fingers itched to follow the path of her gaze, and she shoved her hands into her trouser pockets and lifted her eyes back to his.

He arched his eyebrows, obviously amused. Heat flew to her cheeks. *She'd been gaping at him, for Pete's sake. Of course he was amused.*

She straightened her shoulders. "I'd like a word with you."

"Come on in." He swung the door wider and stepped aside so she could enter.

She slipped past him and into the dressing room. Stopping at its center, she swung around to face him. "Did you ad-lib your reviews for effect?"

Jack looked nonplussed. "Excuse me?"

"Dana told me you ad-libbed. She said you didn't read from the TelePrompTer."

"I didn't need to. I knew what I wanted to say." He took a step toward her. "Do you have a problem with that?"

Jill placed her fists on her hips. "Only if you changed your reviews to contrast with mine. Did you?"

"I adjusted my language, that's all."

The blood rushed to her head. "That's all?" she repeated, incredulous. "People are going to decide whether or not to see those pictures because of our reviews. We're journalists. We have a responsibility—"

"You're a journalist, Jill. I went to film school." He closed the remaining distance between them, stopping so close, she had to tip her head back to meet his eyes. "Besides, we're talking about movies here. Not world policy."

"What did you really think of *A Choice for Love?*"

"I thought it was overwrought and overly sentimental. Just like I said."

"But you didn't think it was totally without merit?"

"No." He swept his gaze over her. "But then, I never said it was."

"You all but called it soap-opera junk."

"You did call the Stallone picture junk."

"But I meant it."

"And so did I." He bent his head to hers. His breath stirred against her cheek. She felt the heat of his body even though they didn't touch. "You know what the real problem here is, Jill? You can't stand to have anyone disagree with you."

"That's not true!"

"It is true." She made a move to step away from him, but he caught her arm, stopping her. "That's why you wanted to review with Clayton. It would have been so comfortable. You could have been the leader, the one in control. Everything could have been your way."

"I wanted to review with Clayton because I respect him."

Jack's eyes narrowed. "Because his opinions are the same as yours. My comment stands."

"You're despicable."

"I'm honest."

"Honest? With whom, Jack? Not with me. Certainly not with yourself."

"What are we talking about now, Jilly? The show? Or the past?"

She jerked up her chin and glared at him. "Take your hand off me."

"So we are talking about the past now. Fine." He tightened his fingers. "I was honest with you, Jilly. Brutally honest. But that wasn't good enough. You wanted me to lie to you. You wanted me to tell you something I didn't, and couldn't, feel. And I'm sorry about that. But I was honest."

"I loathe you, Jack Jacobs. I don't know how I ever got involved with you."

His eyes darkened and a muscle jumped in his jaw. He drew her against his chest. "You've been waiting five years to say that. Feel better now? Or would you like to say it again?"

She curled her hands into fists on his chest. "Once will do, thanks. But I'd really feel better if I never had to see you again."

"I don't think that's what you want at all. His voice deepened, and he looked at her mouth for one heady moment. When he lifted his gaze to hers, she saw something strong and hot in his eyes. Anger. Awareness. The kind of intimacy that's never severed, even after the relationship that created it is.

Despite everything, or maybe because of it, she knew this man better than any other, even than the man who had been her husband.

And he knew her just as well.

He bent his head toward hers, his eyes dark with emotion. "Either hit me or kiss me, Jilly. That's what you want."

Beneath her hand she felt the wild beat of his heart, the heat of his skin. Her knees turned to putty. She tugged against his grasp. "Don't flatter yourself. You don't affect me that much one way or another."

He pulled her closer. "You're a poor liar, Jill Lansing."

"And you're an insufferable son-of-a—"

"Which is it going to be? Are you going to hit me or . . ." He lowered his eyes to her mouth again, and the feeling she'd been fighting took her by storm.

She flexed her fingers against his chest, fighting the awareness, his skin hot and firm under hers. "I don't want to kiss you," she whispered, her husky voice making her words laughable. "And I don't believe in violence."

He inched her even closer. Her arms wedged between them hardly lessened the contact of their bodies. "Hit me or kiss me," he said again.

He lowered his mouth until it hovered over hers. She made a sound of arousal. Of pain. She did want to kiss him, so badly, she trembled with the need. All she would have to do was lift her face a fraction of an inch, and she would feel his mouth against hers. Again, finally, after all these years. She would be able to taste him. To lose herself in him.

Lose herself in him.

The way she had five years ago. And once again she would be opening the door to a world of pain. Jack Jacobs would hurt her now, just as he had before.

She didn't have only herself to think of now.

Rebecca.

Thoughts of her daughter, Peter, and her upcoming appointment with the lawyer filled her head—and cleared it. She couldn't afford to lose herself in Jack, or in anyone or anything else. She had Rebecca to think of.

She stiffened. "Let me go, Jack. Now."

"It's what you really want?"

"Yes." She cleared her throat. "Yes," she repeated, "it's what I want."

For the space of a heartbeat he remained immobile. Then he dropped his hands and took a step away from her. "Fine."

She didn't move. She felt bereft without his warmth, without his hard body to lean against. Her hands tingled from where they'd been pressed against his naked chest, her mouth ached with the need to meet with his.

Regret, both bitter and sweet, moved over her, even as she squared her shoulders and lifted her chin. In the last five years her life had changed; she had changed. This time she wouldn't fall under Jack's spell. "Don't touch me again," she said softly. "Your right to do so ended a long time ago."

He slipped his hands into the front pockets of his blue jeans. "Afraid if there's a next time you won't be able to lie about the way you feel?"

He'd read her mind.

Cursing him silently, she turned and, without acknowledging his comment, walked out of the dressing room.

THREE

Jack stood outside Jill's townhouse complex, hands tucked into the back pockets of his denims, his eyes lifted to her lit windows. Today he'd proved himself both a liar and a fraud. When he'd agreed to do *Reel Reviews*, he'd told himself that being with Jill wouldn't affect him, that this time around he would be able to keep his eyes and his energies fixed firmly on his goals.

What a joke. He'd found himself watching her as she moved around the studio, found himself listening for her voice, her laughter, had found his thoughts consumed by her. He made a sound of self-derision. He'd behaved like a lovestruck adolescent.

Same as he'd always acted around Jill Lansing.

Jack shook his head. And like an adolescent he'd found himself pushing at her, determined to break through her cool, professional veneer, determined to prove to her that she still felt something for him. Determined, perversely, to prove to her that walking out on him had been a mistake.

Even though he'd never doubted that her leaving had been the best thing for them both.

She moved across one of her windows, and he sucked in a quick, sharp breath, arousal kicking him squarely in the gut. What was her power over him? Why did just a glimpse of her affect him like a stunning punch to his solar plexus?

Their past.

It had never been resolved, not really. She had walked out of his life, and their relationship had been over. No long, painful death. No final angry resolution. No time to adjust to its ending.

In a strange way he still thought of her as his lover. His body still reacted to her that way. The thought of her with another man, even the one she had been married to, affected him the way red affected a bull.

He swore. This was crazy. He wasn't her lover. He had no claim on her, no right to be jealous. They had to work together. Amicably. For the good of the show and their careers. Jack frowned. He couldn't be wanting to kiss her. He couldn't have himself pushing her to want to kiss him. He couldn't have them fighting.

Their fights had always led to the same thing—making love.

He swallowed hard, memories swamping him, his senses. Memories of Jill in his arms, naked and satisfied; her mouth on his; her murmured sounds of pleasure. Memories of the way she had looked at him while he loved her—as if he were the only man in the world.

Scowling, Jack shook the memories off. He'd come to see Jill tonight to apologize for this afternoon. To offer her a truce. An offer to try to talk it out. Maybe if they talked, they could put the past, and the seething feelings between them, to rest.

Considering his behavior in his dressing room today, he wouldn't be surprised if she tossed him out on his ear.

Dammit. He'd wanted to kiss her so badly, he'd been able to taste her. He'd wanted her in his arms, his bed. He had wanted to make love with her.

She'd wanted him just as much. He drew in a deep, cleansing breath. But just as he'd known that kissing her, wanting her, was a mistake, she'd known it too. He'd seen it in her eyes, had felt it in the way she'd clung to him with an angry desperation.

An affair with her would be disastrous. He would be a fool to forget the lessons of the past. He was an adult, intelligent, strong-willed, in control of his emotions and libido.

If he put his mind to it, he could ignore this thing between them. No problem.

He muttered another oath. Then why had he done such a damn poor job of it so far?

That changed tonight, he vowed, striding across the flagstones to the central entryway's gate. Jill's complex consisted of groupings of three two-story townhouses, connected by an entryway and courtyard. Victorian in flavor and painted in muted pastels, the upscale townhouses were at once severe and whimsical.

He rang her buzzer. She answered after a moment, and her thick, sleepy voice moved through his head like a fine, old wine. He reminded himself of his vow and steeled himself against the sensation.

"It's me. Jack. We need to talk."

She hesitated. "Now's not a good time, Jack."

There'd been a time she would have welcomed him

with open arms, no matter what the circumstances. A time when he would have heard happiness instead of hesitation in her voice. The truth of that tore at him, and he called himself a fool.

"I just want to talk, Jilly. About today. About the show."

She hesitated only a moment more, then agreed. "I'll buzz you in."

Seconds later he swung the gate open and stepped into the central courtyard. Perfumed by the abundance of flowers, lit only by garden spots and the reflective light from the resident's windows, the small courtyard had an exotic, secluded feel. In the daytime it would be cool and quiet; at night, with its dark corners and shadowed benches, a place for lovers.

He crossed to Jill's townhouse, reaching it as she opened the door. She wore a rose-colored robe, cinched at the waist. Made of some slippery, silky fabric, it draped her body, hinting at curves without openly displaying them. Her feet were bare, her hair tousled.

She looked too damn tempting and touchable for the conversation he wanted to have.

He forced his eyes back to hers. "Hello, Jilly."

"Jack."

"I hope I didn't wake you?"

She shook her head and shifted her gaze. "I was working." She stepped back from the door. "Come in."

He did and looked around her tastefully decorated foyer and living room, a sense of déjà vu pulling so strongly at him that it took his breath. She'd bought the oyster-colored leather sofa right before they'd moved in together, the matching chair and the brass and glass coffee table right after. The softly patterned throw pillows were new, although they'd had something similar; the landscape hanging above the fireplace bore a striking resemblance to the one hanging above his, the one they'd bought together.

But he saw differences too. Big ones. A child lived here. Toys littered the floor and shelves, a huge basket in the corner spilled over with them; in front of the TV a lopsided tower of children's videotapes looked ready to topple.

Jill followed his gaze. "Sorry about the mess. I haven't had a chance to pick up since Becky went to bed."

He forced a nonchalant smile, a strange tightness in his chest. "You weren't expecting company. Besides, you've seen my place at its worst."

She smiled, though he could see she fought it. "Yours was the quintessential bachelor's pad."

"Until you moved in." He regretted the words; they were too loaded with memories. She felt the same; he could tell by the way she looked away, by the color that inched up her cheeks.

He swore silently. Nothing would muddy the conversation and cloud their judgment faster than references to the past.

He cleared his throat. "I didn't come here to dredge up ancient history, Jill. I came to talk about the show."

"So you said." She motioned to the couch. "Have a seat. Would you like a cup of coffee? A drink?"

"Coffee would be great."

"You still take it black?"

He nodded and she went to the kitchen, returning in moments with two steaming mugs.

"It's decaf," she said, crossing the room. She bent

and handed him a mug. As she did, her robe's vee neck gaped slightly, and he caught a glimpse of the creamy, swell of one breast, the hint of a rosy nipple. A jolt of arousal shot through him.

He jerked his eyes back to hers. In her eyes he saw an answering shock of awareness; he saw surprise. He swallowed hard, his mouth suddenly as dry as ash. If he reached up and slipped his hands into the vee of her robe and cupped her, would her nipples pebble against his palms? Would she moan and arch into him as she would have five years ago?

Jack caught himself lifting a hand to find out, and instead curved his fingers around the hot mug, taking it from her outstretched hand. "Thank you," he managed, his voice thick, strained.

Jill straightened, her free hand going to the robe's neckline, adjusting it. "You're welcome," she said stiffly, turning from him, her cheeks bright with color. She crossed to the chair, sank onto it, and curled her legs under her.

She didn't meet his eyes. She gazed into her coffee; he turned his attention to the window and the night beyond.

For several moments they didn't speak. The clock on the mantle ticked out each passing second, so loud in the otherwise silent room that the sound seemed to ricochet off the walls. The sound of traffic from the Pacific Coast Highway drifted through the open windows, along with the cool fall breeze.

He cleared his throat. "This is damn awkward. The whole thing. Sitting here. Working together."

She met his gaze, looking relieved. "Yes, it is."

He laced his fingers around the coffee cup. "But as I see it, it doesn't have to be."

She set aside her coffee and folded her hands in her lap. "Go on."

"We're two people who happen to have a past. But what matters is the present. And the future." He stood and walked to the window. The black night stared silently, mockingly, back at him. He brought the mug to his lips and took a swallow of the hot, bitter drink.

"I came to apologize," he said finally, without turning. "For this afternoon. I was out of line."

He heard the rustle of her robe as she shifted. "I wasn't the picture of professionalism myself."

"I'd like us to call a truce." He turned and met her eyes. "We have to work together. We both want the show to be a success."

"And you're going to do everything you can to see that it is?"

"Yes." He searched her face. Five years ago she had looked at him with passion in her eyes. Always. Now her expression was cool, guarded. He couldn't quite quell his disappointment, his longing for the past and what he had thrown away. "Aren't you?"

She nodded. "I helped conceive *Reel Reviews*. It's important to me."

"Good." He took another swallow of coffee, tamping back the impatience that surged through him. The frustration. "We should be able to do this, then."

"I assume you have a plan."

"Yeah, I have a plan. It's called civil conversation. We put the past behind us."

She looked as if he'd slapped her. He saw her struggle for control. "What?"

"Nothing."

"I said something that upset you."

"No." She shook her head. "So, we put the past behind us. Just like that?"

"I know I can do it."

"Terrific. So can I." She inched her chin up a fraction, the look in her eyes hot and angry. "Why don't we start now? We need to have a civil conversation about the show." She rose and crossed to stand beside him, looking him in the eye. "I don't want you to manipulate your reviews for effect."

He narrowed his eyes. "Are you telling me how to do my job?"

"We're a team here. We have a vested interest in the show's success. And I think what you did today was cheap and dishonest."

"I disagree. And I'm offended."

She flushed and inched her chin up another notch. "You're the one who opened up this conversation, not me."

"I came to try to talk some sense into you about—"

"Sense into me!" She took a step toward him. "I'm perfectly sensible. You're the one who's apologizing here."

"Not for my reviews. They were right on." He closed the distance between them, moving so close, she had to tilt back her head to look at him. "Don't you get it? It doesn't really matter what we say about the movies, it's how we say it. It's getting people to watch us. We're not selling those movies, Jill. We're selling our show."

"But if we're not honest, we're not reviewers. We're circus performers. I didn't go to school to be a performer. It's not what I do."

She started to turn away from him, but he caught her elbows, stopping her. "I didn't change my reviews, Jill. I only reworded them. The Stallone picture wasn't a great film, but it was a hell of a lot of fun. And in my opinion *A Choice for Love* was completely overbaked."

He dropped his hands and stepped back. "The fact is we were great today. And you know it. But you didn't like it because you felt out of control. And your whole life, because of your parents, you've needed to be in control."

Jill's heart began to thrum. "That was low. Even for you, Jack."

"It's true." He lowered his voice. "You've always had to have everything your way. Everything. No compromises. Again, something you learned from your parents."

She stiffened, defensive. "What about your parents, Jack? What about your childhood?" This time it was he who tried to turn away, she who caught his arm. "You know what? I can't even guess. Isn't that sad? All the time we spent together, and I don't even know who you are."

He gazed at her, his jaw tight, anger surging through him. "But you wanted us to be together anyway, right? Up until the moment you decided it was time to walk out." He laughed, the sound hard and icy. "Control, Jilly. With you, it always comes down to who's going to win."

She drew her hand back, as if stung. "So this is your idea of a truce? Of making civil conversation? Going straight for the jugular."

"Hey, I don't see you pulling any punches."

"No, I guess I'm not." She turned away from him and folded her arms.

He gazed at her, at the stiff line of her back and shoulders, and regret moved through him. "Hell, Jilly. I'm sorry."

She shook her head. "Forget it. It's not your fault. It's us. We weren't able to have a civil conversation when we were lovers, I don't see why we should expect to be able to have one now. We always—"

"Mommy?"

They both swung toward the living room doorway. A little girl stood there, clutching a stuffed bunny rabbit in one hand and sleepily rubbing her eyes with the other.

Jill rushed toward her. "Becky, baby, what are you doing up?"

"I thought I heard Daddy." The youngster shifted her gaze to Jack, then looked shyly away. "Daddy here?"

"No, baby," Jill murmured, her voice thick. She cleared her throat and scooped up her daughter. "This is Mr. Jacobs. He and Mommy work together."

The girl peeked at him again, then buried her face in Jill's neck. "How come Daddy isn't here?"

Jack looked at Jill. Her expression was strained, trying to keep him—and her daughter—from seeing how she felt. He opened his mouth to murmur something, he wasn't sure what, but Jill shook her head, stopping him.

"Excuse me," she whispered. "I need to put Becky to bed."

Jack watched her go, his chest tight, a dozen different emotions churning inside him. Jill had looked so hurt when Rebecca had asked for her father, so vulnerable. He remembered the way the child had curled herself around her mother, the way she had pressed her face into Jill's shoulder. And the way Jill had responded. With a fierce protectiveness. Looking at her, he had felt how much she loved her daughter; he'd had a glimmer of what she'd felt all those years ago when she'd thought she was pregnant.

Jack started in the direction Jill had gone, moving down the short hallway. He told himself to butt out, he told himself that what he was doing was an intrusion, but even as the admonitions ran through his head, he stopped in the doorway of the child's room.

Jill sat on the edge of her daughter's bed, and as he watched, she carefully tucked the covers around the girl, then lovingly stroked her hair. All the while she murmured soft, comforting words, ones he couldn't make out and didn't care to—the sound of them told him everything.

A lump formed in his throat. He'd known that Jill had become a mother. Through the grapevine he had heard of her marriage, her pregnancy, her divorce. But he hadn't understood what those things meant to Jill.

He swallowed hard. Now he did. All it had taken was to see the devotion in her eyes when she looked at her daughter, to hear the tenderness in her voice as she soothed her, to see the love in the way she gently stroked her child's silky hair.

He flexed his fingers, the understanding grabbing him by the throat and squeezing so tightly he couldn't breathe. Jill and Becky were linked in a way he would never understand, in a way he could never be a part of.

As if suddenly becoming aware of his presence, Jill turned her head and met his eyes. He read the surprise there, the questions, the affront at his invasion.

He had no place here. He had no part of her daugh-

ter or in their lives. The truth of that affected him like a
swift punch to the gut, and he wheeled around and
strode to the living room. He'd intruded on a private
moment between mother and daughter. A moment that
had nothing to do with him and never would.

Rebecca could have been his child.

But she wasn't.

Pushing the thought, with its conflicting, uncomfortable emotions, away, he crossed to the mantle and
looked at the pictures that lined it. Pictures of Rebecca
—as a baby in Jill's arms, as a young toddler, what
looked to be her first Easter, a recent Christmas, with
Jill's parents.

None included anyone who could be Rebecca's father, although that fact didn't surprise him. Jack drew
his eyebrows together. He'd always wondered what the
man looked like, had always thought of him as an enemy,
a rival, and he would have liked to have an image to go
with his emotions.

"Jack?"

He turned slowly to meet Jill's gaze. At her troubled
expression a lump formed in his throat again. He cleared
it. "I'm sorry, Jilly. I acted on impulse. I had no right."

"No, you didn't." Her words were thick, and she
clasped her hands together. "I think you should go
now."

He knew she was right. He'd stayed too long already;
he'd come tonight to become less involved with her, not
more.

Calling himself a fool, he crossed to stand before her.
"You look so sad."

"Do I?" She turned her head away, but he caught her
chin and turned her face gently back to his.

"Is everything all right with Rebecca?"

Panic raced into her eyes. Fear. "Everything's fine. She has nightmares sometimes, she misses her . . ."

Daddy. The unspoken word landed heavily between them, leaving a painful silence. Jack filled it. "You always wanted to be a mother, you said you'd be a good one. You are, Jill. I can tell."

Tears of gratitude flooded her eyes, so sweet and helpless, it took his breath. "Thank you," she whispered.

He moved his hand to her cheek. "I'm sorry, Jilly. For earlier. I didn't come here to argue. I didn't come here to hurt you."

It took everything she had not to tip her face into his caress, took every ounce of fortitude she possessed to keep from leaning into him and crying. This was the way it had been between them at the end. They'd fought bitterly, then loved each other desperately. Obsessively. She couldn't allow herself to fall into the patterns of before, no matter how much she wanted to.

"I know. It's just us. We can't seem not to argue." She swallowed and stepped away from him, from his burning touch. "We argued about everything. Remember? Movies. Food. Friends. Our lives were one bloody, emotional battle after another."

"But we laughed too. Remember? We had fun together."

She shook her head. "Not at the end. We'd hurt each other too much by then. At the end the only thing we had going for us was great sex."

His expression tightened, and he turned and crossed to the window. For a long time he said nothing, and she gazed at his stiff back, her chest heavy and aching. He looked so alone standing there against the dark rectangle of glass. Invincible yet unbearably vulnerable.

She took an involuntary step toward him, then stopped and drew in a steadying breath. Letting him in tonight had been madness. Thinking they could ever have peace between them was crazier still. They would forever be adversaries.

And they would forever hurt each other. For in that moment she realized that their relationship had hurt him too. She'd never thought so before. She had always believed him to have been left unscathed by their parting.

As if reading her thoughts, he turned and met her eyes. His were dark with regret. "Did you ever love me, Jilly?"

He murmured the question so softly, she thought she might have misheard. His expression told her she hadn't. "You know I did."

"Do I?" He closed the distance between them and cupped her face in his palms once more. "You married so quickly after . . . us."

Heart thundering, she searched his expression. *In his way he had cared for her.* The truth of that barreled over her, stealing her ability to think, to coolly reason. To protect herself.

She wetted her lips. "It was time to move on. It was time to begin my future."

He tightened his fingers. "Were your feelings for me only about your desire to be a mother . . . to have a husband and a family?"

"No!" She shook her head again, vehemently. "How could you ask that? How—"

He moved his hands into her hair, twining his fingers

in it, cupping the back of her head. "I know it was more than sex between us. A lot more."

She made a sound of pain. She wanted to tell him he was wrong, that for her, sex had been the sum total of their relationship. But that would be a lie. She wouldn't have loved him so desperately—or been hurt so badly when she'd realized the truth about them—if the only thing that was between them had been physical.

"Then what was it?" she asked, her voice low and urgent, swamped with tears. "Tell me what it was. Because I haven't a clue."

The expression in his eyes was dark and desperate. "I don't know. Dammit, I—" He bit the words back and lowered his face until it hovered a fraction from hers.

She sucked in a sharp, expectant breath, her pulse scrambling, her nipples hardening, pressing against the silk of her robe. She fisted her hands against his chest. "Tell me, Jack. Tell me what it was."

He swore again, then caught her mouth in a bruising kiss. Stunned, she flattened her hands against his chest, then curled them into the light weave of his sweater, holding on as tightly as she would to a roller coaster during its most daring, most breathtaking spiral of all.

Like a roller-coaster ride there was nothing soft about the kiss. Nothing gentle, nothing that coaxed. It stole her breath and ability to think. It rearranged her insides and scared her senseless.

Then he let her go, so suddenly, she would have stumbled had she not clutched his sweater. She looked at him, stunned and panting.

"You could have been the best thing that ever happened to me," he muttered, his voice fierce. "That's the one thing I am sure of."

"Could have been?" Shaking, she tightened her fingers in his sweater, afraid if she let him go, she wouldn't have the strength to stand.

"If I had let you. If you hadn't walked out."

She bit back a sound of pain. "I walked out because I realized our relationship would never go anywhere. Because I wanted a future, not a dead end."

He took a step away from her, forcing her to drop her hands. "Obviously. You were married within six months."

Anger at the accusation in his tone surged through her. "Like that mattered to you. Give me a break. You never wanted me, Jack. You never wanted to make a commitment to me."

"I couldn't make a commitment to you, Jilly. There's a difference." He flexed his fingers, his jaw tight with control. "It's who I am. And yeah, it has to do with my family. My childhood.

He crossed to the door, turning back to her when he reached it, the expression in his eyes hard and cold. She could hardly believe he was the same man who had just held her with such passion, who had just kissed her with such heat.

She hugged herself, battling the tears. "Seems pretty dumb to throw away something that could have been the best thing that ever happened to you."

For several moments he stared at her. Then he shook his head. "So now you know a little more about me. Good night, Jilly."

He shut the door softly behind him. Jill stared at it for a moment, then with a sound of pain, sank onto the couch and cried.

❦

Jack made the trip home from Jill's at a speed that would have landed him in jail had he been caught. As he swung his car into the driveway, he realized he'd been gripping the steering wheel so tightly, his fingers were numb. As numb as he was inside.

Jill had a child. She was a mother.

Until tonight that fact hadn't been real to him. Until he'd seen the youngster's sweet, sleepy face, Jill's motherhood hadn't been real to him. She'd had a baby with another man. There was a piece of her that he would never, could never, be a part of.

He rested his head against the seat back, Rebecca's image filling his head—hair the color of Jill's, rumpled from sleep; big, dark eyes; a shy smile and high, childish voice.

His gut tightened, and he gripped the steering wheel harder. Rebecca could have been his child—but she wasn't. She belonged to another man. Jill had belonged to another man.

He muttered an oath, Jill's words running crazily through his head, taunting him.

"Seems pretty dumb to throw away something that could have been the best thing that ever happened to you."

Not dumb. Not crazy.

Survival.

Muttering an oath, Jack swung the car door open and stepped out. He crossed to his front door and let himself in to his empty house. He flipped on the light, then headed to the kitchen in search of a beer. He dug one out of the box, opened it but didn't drink. He leaned against the closed refrigerator door, his thoughts filled with his past and his father.

Jack moved his gaze over his spacious kitchen and beyond, to the living room. What would his father think of his place? he wondered. What would he think of the life he had created for himself? His house was typical of California, an open floor plan with an abundance of windows and several skylights, but not particularly big or fancy. The colors and furnishings reflected a southwestern influence, and he'd collected several nice pieces of Indian art and textiles, but nothing of museum quality.

Still, this place was light-years from Trotter Junction, Iowa, and the small, crowded house he and his siblings had grown up in.

Frowning, Jack brought the beer to his lips. Had it really been six years since he'd visited Trotter Junction? He hadn't been counting, but now that he did, he realized it was true. He and Jill had been together then; she had convinced him to go home for his sister Sue's wedding.

So he had gone, and the bitter feud with his father had put a pall over the festivities—even though they'd avoided each other, even though they'd exchanged neither words nor gazes.

While going through her divorce Sue had accused them of hexing the marriage with their bad feelings for each other. Although she'd later apologized, it had hurt him deeply. Because he loved his sister so much. And because he had swallowed his pride so that he could be with her.

He'd never gone back.

He never would.

Jack thought of his father and of the angry, bitter

words they had aimed at each other twelve years ago. His father had told Jack he was going to fall flat on his face, that he would never amount to anything. His father told him not to bother coming back unless it was on his belly, crawling and begging. He had no intention of crawling. Or begging. Not ever.

Jack took a long pull on the beer, the beverage cold and bitter against his tongue. He had talked to his sister, Sue, the week before; she had said the old man's health was failing and had suggested Jack think about making his peace with their father, suggested that perhaps their father was sorry.

Was he? Jack wondered, taking another swig of beer. He doubted it. The only thing Billy Jacobs had ever been sorry about was having knocked up his girlfriend. Jack had been the result, and his father had never tired of reminding Jack that he'd thrown away his dreams for him, that he'd had to give up his music to be a husband and a father.

Jack muttered an oath. Yet when it had come to his own dreams, his father had expected—no, demanded— that his only son do the same. Throw them away. Stay in the one-factory town surrounded by corn, the same town his father had always hated, and be the same thing that had turned his father into such a bitter and beaten old man.

Jack had finally told him what he thought of him and what he could do with his demands, and had left home, striking out on his own. Everything Jack had done, all that he'd achieved, he'd done without family, without help.

He crossed to the sink and gazed at his reflection in the window above it, searching for a resemblance to his father, looking for the grim set of the mouth and jaw, the weary droop of shoulders, the glint of bitterness in the eyes. Jack drew his eyebrows together. He saw none of those; he'd vowed he never would.

He would never become the man Billy Jacobs had become. He would never give up on his dreams.

Jill.

The image of her moved through his head, bringing with it longing and regret, both so strong, he ached with them. Jack turned away from the window and his reflection, crossed to the light switch, and flipped it off.

He would never become the man his father was. No matter what he had to sacrifice in the process.

FOUR

Jill gazed up at the makeup artist, a crazy-looking girl named Mandee, and made a sound that was both amused and sympathetic. "Man trouble, huh?"

"As always." The girl sighed. "They're all devils. If I wasn't so nuts about 'em, I'd never have anything to do with one again. Tip your head back, please."

Jill did as Mandee requested, and the girl sighed again. "They turn you and your world upside down and backward, then look at you with big bedroom eyes and ask what's bugging you. Really! I mean, what are they thinking?"

Jill didn't answer, but then Mandee didn't expect her to. She shut her eyes, and the artist smoothed a cool, tingling lotion around them. Mandee was a talkative woman, and usually Jill halfway tuned her out. But this morning the girl had hit on something Jill could relate to and agree with—all men were devils, especially Jack, her ex-husband, and the lawyer she had an appointment with after the show.

The lawyer. Jill recalled her phone conversation with

him, and her chest tightened. *"This is the nineties, Ms. Lansing. Judges are routinely awarding custody to fathers. There's always a chance the judge could rule in favor of your ex-husband.*

A chance she could lose Rebecca. How would she be able to stand it?

"Relax your facial muscles, please. You're frowning."

"Sorry," Jill murmured, struggling to do what Mandee asked. She turned her thoughts away from her daughter; they landed on Jack.

The week since he'd come to her townhouse had been busy. She'd had her column to do, movies to see and review, the show to prepare for. Her mother had been in town on business, and she and Rebecca had spent an evening with her. Peter's threat and her scheduled meeting with the lawyer had been hanging over her head, and Rebecca had caught her first cold of the fall.

Even with all that she'd been unable to expel Jack from her thoughts. She'd tried, reminding herself of the bad times, of how much he had hurt her, reminding herself of her vow never to get involved with a man like Jack again. She'd gone over what she needed in a man, in a relationship. Someone who would want to be a father and a husband, someone who would give her the love she had always yearned for. She'd reminded herself that she would never have any of those things with Jack.

None of it had worked. Thoughts of him had even invaded her sleep, creating desperate, erotic dreams. Those dreams had blended weirdly with ones of Rebecca and Peter and the custody battle to come. Every morning she'd awakened still fatigued and achy; she hadn't had a good night's sleep in a week.

And thirty minutes from now she would have to face

Jack in front of television cameras. Thousands would see her every reaction to him, her every expression. A wave of nerves rolled over her, and she breathed in deeply through her nose. She would have to behave in a cool, professional manner; she would have to act as if he were no more than a colleague and fellow reviewer.

She would have to act as if he hadn't kissed her one week ago—and as if she wasn't dying for him to kiss her again.

She curled her fingers into fists. How could the simple brush of one person's mouth against another's be so cataclysmic? So earth-shattering?

Simple? The brush of a mouth?

Dear God, there'd been nothing simple, nothing light about the touch of his lips against hers. He'd possessed her mouth boldly. He'd dominated it. And she had fallen under the spell of his kiss as quickly, as easily, as she had five years ago.

"You're frowning again."

"Sorry. Again."

Jill smoothed her features. More than the memory of his kiss had plagued her since that night. She'd been unable to forget the bleak expression in his eyes when he'd said good-bye. She'd been unable to put his words from her mind. *"You could have been the best thing that ever happened to me . . . if I'd let you."*

Those words had replayed in her head, over and over, taunting her. If only he hadn't told her that. If only he had left well enough alone. If only she hadn't turned away from Rebecca's bed and found him gazing at them, the expression in his eyes bittersweet with longing.

It had been more than chemistry between them. It had been emotional.

He had cared for her.

Not enough, she reminded herself. Not with the depth that she had cared for him. But it had been something . . . he had *felt* something for her. She'd been special to him.

"Frown like that again, Ms. Lansing, and I refuse to be responsible for the results."

"I won't." Jill met the other woman's eyes. "Talk to me, Mandee. Tell me about some of the people you've worked on."

Needing no further encouragement, Mandee launched into a story about a well-known soap star and the time he had enlisted her help in juggling his three girlfriends when they had all showed up unexpectedly at the studio. Amusing and fascinating, the artist's story kept Jill's mind off Jack, and in what seemed like no time at all, Jill was sitting beside Jack in front of the cameras.

"I'm sorry," Jill said hotly, facing Jack, "but Bill Pleasant's script has about as much heart as a steamroller. I can't believe you call this a woman's movie."

Jack smiled arrogantly. "I'm sure I'm not the only critic who'll call it that. After all, it's primarily a romance. Boy meets girl, boy wants girl, boy gets girl—"

"A romance?" she interrupted, tossing her hair over her shoulder. "By whose standards? And think about your language, Jack. The main protagonist is a male. The action of the story revolves totally around his needs, his goals. So tell me how this can be woman's movie?"

He shook his head. "Okay, so call it a relationship movie. Demographically speaking, traditionally considered a woman's territory." He gestured with his hands. "What about the scene in the café when they first encounter each other? Their eyes meet, and you can see the chemistry between them. It's so potent, you could cut it with a knife. If that's not romance, Jill, what is?"

Jill recalled the highly sexed scene and shuddered. Looking at Jack now, she could imagine it had been the two of them in that situation; their relationship had begun in a similar fashion. And look where it had taken them.

"That's not love, it's lust. It's a male's version of romance." She smiled sweetly. "But then you obviously don't know the difference."

Her barb struck its mark, she saw, by the slight tightening of his mouth, by the flicker of emotion in his eyes. He leaned forward, his smile more than a little dangerous. "Maybe I never had the right teacher. You want the job, Ms. Lansing?"

Her pulse scrambled; a flush started at her toes and moved upward until she felt as if her entire body was aflame. She stiffened her spine against the sensation. "In your dreams, Jacobs. I'd rather give those kinds of lessons to a snake."

"I've been called worse."

"I don't doubt it." She flashed him another smile, then turned toward the camera. "Next up, from the director of *Laughingstock* and *Nerds in Space*, a comedy about being dead."

The rest of the show passed in a similar fashion, and by the time they'd reviewed all four movies, Jill was torn between a myriad of conflicting feelings and urges. He made her angry; he excited her. She wanted to hit him; she wanted to kiss him. She wanted to quit the show; she wanted to argue her points until she proved to him and the entire L.A. area that he was wrong.

Unfortunately, none of those reactions were appropriate, and she had nowhere to put the surplus of adrenaline racing through her. She stood and smoothed her skirt with an outward calm that surprised even her. Smiling and thanking the various crew members she passed, she walked off the set.

She drew in a deep, calming breath, gathering her thoughts. Her heart slowed, her pulse steadied and reason returned. She was in control here, she told herself. Of the show. Her feelings. Her behavior. What had happened during taping was simply the result of . . . What?

Professional stimulation. Sure. Although it was frustrating working with Jack, doing *Reel Reviews* was exciting. This was an incredible opportunity. A once-in-a-lifetime chance. This was . . .

Hogwash.

She frowned. The truth was their banter had excited her. It had been full of innuendo. It had crackled with their physical awareness. She had wanted to show him up almost as badly as she'd wanted to touch him. And when his gaze had met hers, she had seen the same longing in his eyes.

This thing between her and Jack was strong. Overpoweringly so. It pulled and pushed at her, breaking through all her defenses. When she was with Jack, all her vows and determined intentions fell away, leaving her exposed, vulnerable, and aching for him.

The same as it always had.

No one else had ever affected her that way. Not even the man who had been her husband. Guilt and regrets washed over her. Peter had accused her of not loving him enough, of not loving him as much as she had loved Jack.

She had denied that hotly. Again and again.

Had Peter been right? Had she herself been to blame for the end of her marriage? Jill flexed her fingers, wanting to deny any culpability. She'd been a good wife. A good mother. She'd given her marriage one hundred percent of her energy. She'd—

Never forgotten Jack.

The truth of that took her breath away. Peter hadn't been completely off base. Instead of jealously fabricating her yearning for Jack, maybe . . . just maybe, he had felt it.

That hurt. Badly. If it were true, then she had been less than honest with Peter. With herself. If it were true, she had never given her marriage one hundred percent.

And now if she didn't watch her step, she would be in deep trouble. She acknowledged that truth, even as her stomach sank. Watching her step, when it came to Jack, shouldn't be so difficult. He'd hurt her. Terribly. She and Jack wanted opposite things from life; they had no future together. She was old enough to know better, old enough to be able to follow her head instead of her heart.

But she'd tried that too. She had followed her head, and look where it had taken her—first into a bitter divorce, now a custody battle for Rebecca. *Her sweet Becky, what would she do if she lost her?* Panic tugged at her, and she fought against it. She couldn't fall apart, not now.

"Terrific show," Dana said, coming up behind her.

Jill pushed aside her worries and turned slowly to face her friend. "You didn't think we needed to retape anything? Not even the part when I—"

"Especially not that part." Dana laughed at Jill's expression. "It's going to take you a little while to get used to this, isn't it?"

"I suppose it is." A smile pulled at her mouth, and Jill tucked her hair behind her ear. "I'm glad you're pleased."

"Tim and I are talking about making a few adjustments to the format. We'd like to discuss them with you and Jack." She checked her watch. "Could you come to my office in a—"

"Great show, Lansing." Jack ambled over, his expression amused. "I especially liked the part when you called me a snake. Nice touch."

She laughed. "Don't you worry, I meant every word."

"I was afraid of that." He turned to Dana. "What did you think?"

"That it was great. But as I was just telling Jill, I'd like us to meet in my office in an hour. We need to powwow a couple of changes we're planning to make to the show. Tim and I want you two involved."

"An hour?" Jill repeated, shaking her head, thinking of the lawyer and her dreaded meeting with him. "I can't, Dana. I have an appointment . . . it's too important to postpone." She heard the quiver in her voice and fought to control it. "I could probably be back in an hour and a half."

Jill felt Jack's questioning gaze upon her; she kept her eyes fixed firmly on Dana's face. If she looked at him, she might burst into tears. And that was the last thing she wanted to do—and the last thing he would want from her. He'd made that clear the other night.

Dana checked her watch. "It's okay with me. How about you, Jack?"

He murmured his agreement, and Jill excused herself, not wanting to give either of them a chance to question her.

Jack caught up with her just as she stepped through KTBC's front entrance and into the California sunshine. "Jill, wait."

She turned to face him, saw the questions in his eyes. And concern. She swore silently and looked away. She'd never been able to hide her feelings from him, and she didn't want to get into a discussion about them now—or ever. Not with him anyway.

She forced a smile. "What's up?"

He drew his eyebrows together and searched her expression. "I wanted to make sure you're okay."

"I'm fine," she said quickly. "I'm just late, that's all."

He caught her hand, stopping her again. "You're sure? There's nothing . . . else?"

Her heart lodged in her throat. She longed suddenly to rest her head against his chest and spill out all her fears, longed for him to hold her and comfort her. Only he wouldn't be able to comfort her, he wouldn't be there to support her. He'd proved that before.

She slipped her hand from his and angled up her chin. "Yes, I'm sure. And standing here talking to you is only making me later."

He took a step away from her, a muscle working in his jaw. "Sorry for being concerned," he said tightly. "My mistake."

He turned on his heel and walked away. She watched him for a moment, the longing from seconds ago returning, stealing her ability to move, to think clearly. She started to call after him, then regaining her good sense, turned and headed to her car.

❖━━━❖

Where was she? Jack wondered for what seemed like the hundredth time in the past minutes. He glanced surreptitiously at his watch, not wanting to further remind Dana that Jill was late.

Twenty-five minutes' late. He only half listened to Dana and Tim's conversation. It was unlike Jill to be late; she'd always been punctual to a fault.

Something was wrong.

He'd known it earlier, had seen it in her eyes, in the line of her mouth, had heard it in her voice. He'd let his male pride get in the way of his instincts.

Her cool indifference had been doubly difficult to take, considering that for a week now all he'd been able to do was think of her, of the way her mouth had felt beneath his and his longing to kiss her again.

He never should have given in to the temptation, the delight, of her kiss. He drew his eyebrows together. Damn it to hell. He'd known better at the time; he'd vowed he wouldn't let her turn him inside out and—

"Sorry I'm late." Jill rushed into Dana's office. "My appointment ran long, then traffic was bumper-to-bumper all the way." She hesitated, then took the first available chair—the one directly across from his. "Have I missed much?"

While Dana filled her in, Jack studied Jill. She'd been crying. She'd worked to hide it, but she hadn't been able to completely conceal the redness in her eyes, the slight puffiness around them. Even if she had been able to hide all the traces of her tears, he would still have seen her distress—by her wounded expression. She looked like she might fall apart.

She needed him.

Even as the thought moved through his head, he called himself a fool. She neither needed nor wanted his comfort or protection. She'd made that clear five years ago, and again five nights ago. He would do well to remember that.

He forced his attention to what Dana was saying. He listened to the changes the producer and director wanted to implement, made comments and suggestions, all the while his thoughts on Jill and what might be bothering her.

Dana and Tim brought the meeting to a close. Jill stood and excused herself, claiming another appointment.

Oh, no, you don't, Jack thought, starting after her. Something was going on, and he intended to find out what.

Tim caught him before he reached the door. "Jack, could I have another moment?"

Jack watched as Jill disappeared down the hallway. Swearing silently, he turned to the other man and smiled. "Sure, Tim. What's up?"

Twenty minutes later Jack stepped through KTBC's front entrance and headed toward the parking lot. Even though he knew Jill was no doubt long gone, he looked for her, stopping short in surprise when he saw her white Volvo in line at the exit gate.

Acting on impulse, he sprinted to his car, fishing his keys from his pocket as he ran. He reached the car, climbed in, started it up, and threw it into gear, all in one breath. He didn't know what the hell he hoped to accomplish by following her, but he did it anyway.

He made it to the gate just after she'd driven

through. He followed her at a discreet distance, running a couple of long yellows to keep her in sight. The whole time he tailed her, he called himself a fool. An idiot. He told himself to butt out, to wise up. To drive in the opposite direction.

Instead when she turned into a McDonald's several miles from the station, he followed her, parking his car and watching as she hurried inside. Moments later he saw her step out onto the Playland, greet a young woman, then watched as Rebecca flew toward her and launched herself into her mother's arms.

She'd come to meet Rebecca. He narrowed his eyes to get a better look. The little girl appeared to be fine, happy, and fit. He cocked his head. Jill, on the other hand, clutched her daughter desperately, and she squeezed her eyes tightly shut as she held on to the little girl.

Jill held her daughter as if she was afraid she would never see her again.

Ridiculous.

He frowned. What was wrong with him? He was spying on his former lover and present colleague like some sort of lonely old busybody. Her life and problems were no concern of his. She'd made that clear the day she'd walked out of their relationship without even a good-bye.

Scowling fiercely, he called himself fourteen kinds of fool, swung the car door open, and stepped out into the parking lot. Damn it to hell, he thought, crossing to the restaurant's entrance, he'd never been any good at taking advice, not even his own.

Past the lunch hour but before the dinner rush, the restaurant was nearly empty. He stopped at the counter, ordered a Coke and French fries, then headed out to the children's play area.

Jill sat at one of the first tables, watching her daughter romp in the ball pit. *Last chance to play it smart, Jacobs. Turn around and walk away now.*

Instead he drew a deep breath and crossed to stand beside her. "Fancy meeting you here."

She stiffened and swung slowly to face him. Their eyes met, hers naked with pain. "I didn't know McDonald's Playland was one of your hangouts," she murmured.

He smiled and took the seat across from her. "Gotta have those fries." He popped one in his mouth.

She didn't smile. "Funny you chose this McDonald's, at this exact time."

He grinned. "One of life's little coincidences."

"Mommy! Watch!"

Jill turned toward her daughter, clapping loudly as the youngster flung herself into the sea of balls. A moment later she met his eyes again. "Did you follow me?"

"Yes," he said simply. "I did."

She let her breath out in a shaky rush. "Why? I can't imagine there's anything we have left to say to each other after the other night."

"Mommy!"

Jack followed her gaze to the ball pit and the young girl playing there. She couldn't imagine? What would she say if she knew how she, and now her child, drew him? If she knew how just watching them warmed him? He found himself looking at them the way a freezing man would a brightly lit window.

He shook the thought off. He'd come because he and Jill had had a relationship. And even though the relationship had ended long ago, he still cared for her, as a friend. He still worried about her welfare. And his attraction to mother and daughter together was nothing more than curiosity. Jill had so longed to be a mother that seeing her as one now was . . . interesting. That was all.

He turned back to Jill. "I followed you because I saw that you were upset, and I thought you might . . . need me."

She looked at him, then away, her eyes bright with unshed tears. "I needed you five years ago, I don't now. This is my time with Rebecca. Please go."

He ignored her and watched the children romping in the ball pit. They interacted with one another honestly, not hiding their feelings and needs, not worrying what the other kids might think of them.

He shifted his gaze to Jill's pensive profile. "Do you remember what it was like to have fun like that? To be so free?"

For a moment she said nothing, then she shook her head. "I don't think I was ever so carefree. My childhood was so . . . cold. So . . . quiet." She cleared her throat. "It's one of the things I promised myself I would give Rebecca, a carefree childhood. One full of fun and laughter."

He looked at her. "And one full of love?"

"Yes," she whispered. "Especially love."

He reached across the table and curved his hand over hers. "I hope you never thought my . . . doubts about marriage and parenthood had anything to do with you. You're a good mother, Jill. I always knew you would be."

She slipped her hand from his and stood. "Excuse me, I need to make sure Rebecca—"

"Rebecca's fine." He caught her hand. "Jilly, don't."

She bit her lower lip, struggling, he saw, to keep her feelings hidden. Beneath his, he felt her hand tremble. "Don't what?" she managed, her voice thick.

"Don't shut me out. Don't run away. Tell me what's wrong."

"Please . . . go away. I don't want to fall apart. Not here, not in front of Rebecca."

He caught his breath, a horrible fear, one he'd been harboring since earlier today when she'd said she had an appointment, then later when he'd seen the devastation in her eyes as she'd rushed into the meeting, forcing its way to the front of his thoughts.

He tightened his fingers on hers. "Jilly, are you . . . ill?"

He held his breath as she searched his expression. Her eyes softened, her mouth relaxed, curving up into a soft smile. "No, Jack. I'm fine. As far as I know, I'm healthy as a horse."

The release of tension left him feeling almost light-headed with relief. "I'm glad. I thought . . . that you . . ."

His voice trailed off. She smiled again. "Thank you for worrying."

She looked at Rebecca again. The little girl and another youngster were tossing balls into the air as fast as they could, giggling with delight.

Her small smile faded. "When Peter and I divorced, we set up a temporary arrangement for custody of Rebecca. We both wanted her of course, and it seemed simple and logical just to split her time between us both. Peter has her for two weeks, then I have her for two."

She laced her fingers in her lap. "He only lives in San

Diego, and except for missing her desperately when she's with her father, the arrangement has worked well enough."

"Until now."

"Yes." Jill met his eyes, then looked away, swallowing hard. "Next year Rebecca's going to kindergarten, and she has to live one place or the other."

Dread turned his mouth to ash. He suspected what was coming next, but he asked anyway. "And?"

"And Peter wants full custody." She clasped her hands so tightly in her lap that her knuckles stood out shockingly white against the navy of her skirt. "I can't lose her, Jack. I just . . . can't."

He reached over and covered her clenched hands with his own, aching for her, understanding—with a part of himself that was totally foreign to him—her fear.

He moved his thumb slowly, soothingly, across her knuckles. "But you're her mother, Jill. And you're a good one. Anyone can see that. How much of a chance is there that a judge—"

"Too much of a chance," she whispered, her expression stricken. "At least according to the lawyer I met with this afternoon."

So that's where she had been. He moved his fingers against hers again. "Tell me what he said."

She drew in a deep, shaky breath. Her hand trembled beneath his. "He said that many judges today are deciding in favor of fathers. He said that the judge will look at each of us as parents, at how stable we are, at the home and environment we provide Rebecca.

"You're a good mother," Jack said again fiercely. "You love your daughter so much, no judge in his right mind would separate the two of you."

"I work," she muttered, her voice tight with anger and frustration. "That's a strike against me, don't you know?"

Fury swept through him. "Your ex-husband works. How the hell are you supposed to provide a home for Rebecca if you don't work?"

"Peter's remarried." She curled her fingers around Jack's. "His wife's a full-time mother and homemaker. She makes cookies, and does craft projects, and volunteers at the church. They live in a pretty little house in a neighborhood filled with other kids and other mommies who don't work outside the home." Her mouth tightened. "Some judges, it seems, are unduly impressed by those things."

Jack swore softly and turned to face Jill. "But none of that makes her a better mother than you are. None of those things means she loves Rebecca more than you do."

"I know that, but how do I prove it, Jack? If the judge is predisposed to think those things are most important, how do I prove that they're not?"

Jack made a sound of frustration. "Hell, Jilly, I don't know."

Silence fell between them for a few moments. "My mother was never there for me," Jill finally said. "Her career always came first. She always had a meeting or a sales trip or a dinner with a client. We didn't make cookies or crafts; she wasn't there to clean and bandage my skinned knees or to take care of me when I was too sick to go to school.

"I promised myself I wouldn't be the kind of mother she was. I'm not, but what if "—she shuddered—"what if the judge doesn't see that?"

"Jilly, look at me." The expression in her eyes tore at him. More than anything in the world he wished he could hold and comfort her; he wished he could make everything okay.

"You have a successful career, and so does your mother. The similarity between you ends there. Rebecca is your first priority, and you would do anything for her. I know you, and I know that. I see it now. I saw it the other night."

"But the lawyer said—"

"He's wrong." Anger filled him, and he caught her hand again. "I'd like to string that alarmist bastard up by his toes for scaring you this way."

"Preparing me. I have to know what I'm up against. I have to prepare myself in case . . . I . . . in case—"

Tears choked her once more, and he curved his fingers around hers, a fierce protectiveness surging through him. He wanted to hold her, protect her, slay dragons for her if need be.

"You won't lose her," he said, his voice edged with steel. "It's not going to happen."

"Mommy, I'm thirsty!" Rebecca barreled across the play area, skidding to a stop when she noticed Jack.

Jack smiled. "Hello."

She looked at her mother, then, as if reassured, back at Jack. "I met you before."

"I'm Jack."

Rebecca's eyes crinkled at the corners as she smiled —just the way Jill's did. He breathed past the sudden catch in his chest, and called himself a fool.

"Like the story," the little girl said, climbing onto the seat between him and Jill. "Jack fell down and broke his crown. *Crown* means 'your head.' "

He nodded solemnly. "I did hear something about that."

"It's true." Rebecca eyed his tray. "Can I have some French fries?"

Jack looked to Jill. "If it's okay with your mom."

" 'May I have a French fry, please?' " Jill corrected, amusement and affection coloring her tone.

The little girl tipped her face up to his and batted her eyelashes. "May I please have a French fry, Jack?"

He stared at her a moment, completely charmed. Then he smiled and slid the tray toward her. "You may have them all. But I'm afraid they're probably cold by now."

"Don't care," she said, carefully selecting one from the box. "I like my food cold."

Jill touched Rebecca's hair lightly. "She really does. At restaurants I ask the server to put her food in the freezer for a few moments after it's prepared."

"But most times they think she's kidding." Rebecca made a sound of disgust. "Then I have to blow on it. It takes forever."

"That is a bummer."

"Bummer," Rebecca repeated. "Yuk."

She made a face, stuffed a fry into her mouth, and selected another. The other night he hadn't realized how outgoing and precocious Rebecca was. And even though he didn't know much about children, Rebecca seemed bright. Really bright.

"Finish up, sweetie. We need to go."

"How come?"

"It's getting late, and I have some things I need to take care of before dinnertime."

"Can Jack come too?"

Jill made a sound of surprise. "I don't think so."

"Why not?"

"Well . . . I . . . he—" Pink inched over her cheeks. "I don't think he would want to run to the dry cleaner and grocery with us. Would you, Jack?"

He met Jill's eyes. Hers pleaded with him to agree with her. "I'd love to go with you, Rebecca, but I can't this time. Will you invite me another?"

She nodded glumly, looked longingly at the half-full box of French fries, sighed, and pushed them toward him. "Okay."

Jack reached out to tweak her nose, then realizing what he was doing, dropped his hand and slid the tray back to her. "Please take them, Rebecca. I'm finished."

Her face lit up, and she swung toward her mother. "Can I, Mommy? Can I, please?"

" '*May I*,' Rebecca." Jill lifted her eyes to Jack's, the expression in them so filled with love, it stung. "And yes, you may."

FIVE

Two weeks later Jill pulled into KTBC's parking lot, eased into the first available spot, and cut off the Volvo's engine. She flipped down her visor mirror, checked her appearance, and thought of Jack. In the time that had passed since she'd spilled her guts to him at the McDonald's, she had hardly talked to him. Other than the times they'd been forced to be together because of the show, she had avoided him.

Jack had made it easy for her. Since that afternoon at the Playland he hadn't once sought her out, he hadn't teased or tried to charm her, he hadn't made reference to anything that didn't directly have to do with the show. Except during taping, he'd seemed uncomfortable around her, as if he, too, regretted their conversation.

Whatever Jack's reasons for steering clear of her, she'd needed—and appreciated—the distance between them. It had afforded her the time and space to reerect her emotional guards. Letting them down had been a mistake, a big mistake.

Because once they were down, Jack could ease his way back into her heart.

Frowning, she curled her fingers around the steering wheel. What was wrong with her? Why, after all the time that had passed, after everything that had happened between them, was she still so susceptible to him? It was ridiculous, silly and adolescent. Just as was being unable to eat, sleep or concentrate for thinking of him.

She shook her head. With Rebecca at Peter's, she'd had too much time to think, to brood over the past, to worry over the future. When Becky came home, her life would return to its normal, hectic pace. Thoughts of Jack and their past would once again be relegated to her dreams and the darkest hours of the night.

Jill breathed deeply through her nose. Would they? Or was she simply fooling herself, as she had so many times before? It had hurt to see Jack with Rebecca. He'd been so good with her; he'd charmed her daughter as quickly and as easily as he had charmed her all those years ago.

Jack could have been Rebecca's father. Jill drew in a shuddering breath. Once upon a time she had wanted him to be the father of her children, she had dreamed— and prayed—for him to be.

And except for a few dizzying weeks five years before, those prayers and dreams had gone unanswered and unfulfilled.

She'd thought she could change him. She'd thought he would be happy once he'd had time to adjust to the idea of becoming a father.

Jill stepped out of her car, slammed the door, and started across the parking lot. What a fool she'd been. All along he'd told her he never planned to marry, that he never wanted a family. He'd been honest with her—brutally honest—from the very beginning. But she hadn't been listening, not really. She hadn't believed him. She'd thought that if he'd cared for her enough, he would change his mind.

Maybe he would have, *if* he'd ever cared enough.

He hadn't.

She smiled and waved at one of the cameramen as he hurried past, then slid her hands into her blazer pockets. Of course she hadn't been pregnant at all. The home test had been in error; she had been one of the percentages that made up the disclaimer on the back of the box.

If only she'd visited the doctor before she'd told Jack she was pregnant. If only she'd—

She shook her head. If only what? Would she have continued to fool herself? Would she have continued to believe—in her heart—that Jack loved her? That he would come around?

If she had waited, she wouldn't have Rebecca. And having Rebecca was worth any amount of pain.

She climbed KTBC's front steps, then made her way through the double glass doors and took the elevator up to the executive floor.

The receptionist looked up and smiled. "Good morning."

Jill returned her smile. " 'Morning, Annie. Is Dana ready for me?"

"Ready and waiting. I'll tell her you're on your way back."

"Thanks." Jill moved down the hallway, shifting her thoughts to the upcoming meeting. Dana had scheduled this meeting at the last minute and had acted almost secretive about what she wanted to discuss.

She stopped outside the producer's office, took a deep breath, and mentally prepared herself for seeing Jack. They'd been working together over a month now, but her first look at him still affected her like a high-voltage electrical charge.

Ridiculous, she thought, straightening her spine, disgusted with herself. Today would be the day she looked at Jack Jacobs and felt nothing.

Taking another deep breath, she opened the door and poked her head into Dana's office. The producer sat behind her desk, making notes on a yellow legal pad. Jack had not arrived yet.

"Hi. Am I early?"

Dana looked up, smiled, and motioned her inside. "No, you're right on time. Come in and have a seat."

Jill slid into one of the chairs that faced Dana's desk and checked her watch. "Have you heard from Jack?"

"He's not coming. I spoke to him earlier today."

"Oh." Jill frowned. Something in Dana's eyes troubled her—part excitement, part apology. She had the feeling she was not going to like what Dana had to say. "Is something wrong?"

"No." Dana shook her head. "This is good news. Big news. But . . . I thought I should discuss it with you privately."

Jill's stomach sank. "Okay, Dana, you've adequately unsettled me. Just spill it."

Dana grinned. "Sorry about that. You know me, always serious." She folded her hands on top of the desk in front of her. "The station is excited about *Reel Reviews*. Very excited. We feel we have a real winner. And so apparently does the public."

Jill could see that Dana had to work to contain her excitement. Her own pulse began to thrum. "Go on."

"We've only aired four times," Dana continued, "but we've already gotten hundreds of calls and letters." She lifted a mailbag and dumped its contents onto her desk. There were so many letters and postcards, they spilled off the sides of the desk. "Fan mail."

Stunned, Jill stared at the mountain of mail. "All that mail's in response to *Reel Reviews?*"

"Actually it's in response to you and Jack."

"Me and Jack?" she repeated. "What do you mean?"

"I mean, they love you. The two of you, together."

Together. Jill eased back in her chair, a strange sensation in the pit of her stomach.

"Before you say a thing, just listen." Dana picked up a sheaf of papers she had paper-clipped together and began reading:

". . . Jack and Jill are great together! I love tuning in to see the fireworks! . . . When are those two going to stop arguing and kiss? . . . Jack should just kiss her. . . . Get those two together! Don't they see they're perfect together? . . . Where does she get off calling him a chauvinist? . . . Go for it, Jill! I think he's a chauvinist, Neanderthal too. . . . Wow! What a looker that Jack is. If Jill doesn't want him, here's my name and number. . . . Once again woman proves her superiority to man. . . . As usual men have it hands down over women. . . ."

After she read each quote, Dana handed the letter that contained the highlighted passage to Jill. Jill stared at them, not quite believing her eyes.

Dana passed Jill the last one. "I could go on, but

everything else is just another version of what I read you."

"This is . . . incredible," Jill murmured.

"Do you get what's happening here, Jill?" Jill lifted her gaze to meet Dana's. "You and Jack have caught the imagination of the viewing public. They see you as a couple, and they see the show as a sort of romance."

"They see our show as a romance?" Jill shook her head. "But . . . we're just reviewing movies."

"Remember all the hoopla over those coffee commercials a few years back? They were just selling instant coffee."

And ended up becoming a made-for-TV movie and a romantic novelization.

"My God . . . I'm stunned." Jill looked down at the letters, rereading several, heart thundering. "All these people took the time to write . . . it's incredible."

"I know. But they did. And we're getting more calls and letters every day." Dana spread her hands. "There's something there, between you two. It's a spark, a kind of chemistry. The camera picks it up."

"We're a hit," Jill murmured, then smiled. *"Reel Reviews* is a hit."

Dana laughed. "The minute I saw you and Jack together, I suspected that the two of you were going to make something special happen in front of the camera. The first time you two reviewed together, I knew *Reel Reviews* was going to take off like a rocket."

Jill stood and crossed to the window. She touched the glass with her fingertips, struggling to control her conflicting emotions. She felt nervous and excited and totally off balance.

"Given your and Jack's past relationship, I'm sure this whole thing feels strange."

Jill glanced over her shoulder at her friend, grateful for her understanding. "It does. It's so ironic, such a mocking twist of fate. I've worked so hard to fight my reactions to Jack, to fight that damn spark that always seems to be between us. And now . . . I learn it's what the viewers like."

She returned her attention to the window and the brilliant day beyond, drawing her eyebrows together in thought. "Next to Rebecca, nothing's as important to me as the show and its success. And now the very thing making it a success is the same thing I've fought so long."

Dana took a deep breath. "The show aside, Jill, are you so sure you should fight whatever's between you and Jack? Maybe this time you two could work it out."

"No." Jill swung her gaze to meet her friend's once more. "With Jack there's no working it out, because the future will always be a dead end. Trust me on this."

"I'm sorry." Dana took another deep breath. "And I'm sorry I have to be the one to deliver this next news."

Jill searched Dana's expression, her heart beginning to rap against the wall of her chest. "What is it?"

"The station wants you two to be seen together as much as possible."

"Together?" Jill repeated.

Dana looked decidedly uncomfortable now. "We feel it would be good publicity for the show."

Great for the show, but what about her personal peace of mind? Jill curled her fingers into fists. *What about protecting herself? What about Rebecca?*

She stiffened her spine. "What exactly do you mean

by 'as much as possible'? Are you telling me what to do on my personal time?"

"Of course not. We're talking about your professional activities. Movie premieres, station functions, things like that."

"I see."

"There's more. The station has decided to put the advertising and publicity departments fully behind *Reel Reviews*. We're pulling out all the stops. Bus signs and billboards. Thirty- and sixty-second KTBC spots. Newspaper ads, radio. We all believe *Reel Reviews* has a chance at syndication, and we're prepared to do everything we can to make that happen."

Jill crossed to the chair she'd occupied minutes ago and sank into it, stunned. "Syndication?" she repeated breathlessly. "You really think so?"

"Yup." Dana propped herself on the edge of the desk. "The station's already started the ball rolling. We're throwing a welcome party for advertisers, the media, and other industry bigwigs Saturday night, here in the studio. In addition we've arranged for you and Jack to be interviewed by the television reporter from your paper. He'll be calling you today or tomorrow to set up an appointment. The ad guys are already working on the creative for the print and audio campaign, and next week we'll probably need you for a photo session or two." Dana let out a long breath. "So, what do you think? Fabulous, isn't it?"

Was it? Jill wondered. She was delighted that *Reel Reviews* was a success, but what about the added time she would have to spend with Jack?

She thought of the last two weeks, of the way she'd felt every time she'd looked at him, thought of the expression in his eyes when he looked at Rebecca, of the way he'd occupied her mind. And she thought of Peter and the custody hearing.

She looked at the pile of fan mail. *Syndication. Was it really possible?*

She returned her gaze to her friend's, then laughed. "Yes, fabulous. Incredible. It's all my wildest dreams coming true."

"And you're all right about working so closely with Jack?"

"Do I have a choice?"

Dana paused, then shook her head. "No, I guess not."

"Then it's going to be fine. I'll make it work."

The phone awakened her from a deep sleep. Jill reached for it, knocking over her alarm clock as she did. "Hello," she mumbled, pushing the hair out of her eyes.

"Jilly. It's me."

"Jack?" She fumbled for the clock, squinting to read the numbers as she righted it. *Twelve forty-two.* She pulled herself into a sitting position, her heart beginning to pound. "What's wrong? Has something happened to—"

"No. Everything's fine. I just . . ." He cleared his throat. "I couldn't sleep. I've been . . . thinking about you."

"Oh." That one word sounded small and lost in the silence that ensued, but she couldn't think of another to utter. She wound her forefinger around the phone cord and waited.

"Since that day at McDonald's I . . . I've been worried. How are you doing?"

His thick, sleepy voice brought back memories of other midnight calls, of calls when his words would have been ones of passion, not regret. A lump formed in her throat and she swallowed past it. "Okay," she whispered. "Becky's at her father's. I . . . miss her."

"I'm sorry, Jilly."

"You needn't be sorry. You had nothing to do with—"

"I'm sorry about today. About the show." She said nothing, and after a moment he released a pent-up breath. "I know this isn't the direction you wanted the show to take. It isn't how you envisioned it. And I know that in a way Dana's news must have been hard for you to take."

"In a way," she murmured, her chest tight. "But still, it was good news. Great news."

"I wanted you to know I didn't plan to muck things up for you. I didn't intend to change the show's focus."

She squeezed her eyes shut for a moment, his words, their honesty, touching her to the core, healing a small but deep wound. "I know that, Jack. It's us. Together. We changed the show. As much as I wish I could, I can't deny that it's true."

After a moment he laughed, the sound forced and tight. She heard fatigue and melancholy.

"You want to hear something funny, Jilly? I thought doing this thing, the show, was going to be a cinch, a piece of cake. I thought that I . . . that you would have no effect on me."

He drew in a ragged breath. "I was wrong. I can't sleep, can't concentrate, can't . . ." He swore softly. "I still want you. Still want to make love with you. As strongly as I ever did. Even though I know it's wrong for both of us."

His words hit her like a physical blow. *He wanted her. As much as she did him; as much as he ever had.*

Warmth bloomed inside her. "Jack . . . I—"

"Don't say anything, Jill. We both know there's nothing left to say."

Even knowing he was right, so many words jumped to her tongue. Yet she knew uttering them would change nothing.

The silence stretched between them, filled only with the sound of their breathing, the thunder of her own heart.

Finally, when she thought she might scream, he muttered another oath. "You were right the other night. We were over a long time ago. Even before you walked out on me, maybe from the start."

She gripped the phone cord tightly and waited, her chest aching.

"It wasn't you, Jilly. I want you to know that. It was me. I did keep you at arm's length."

"Why?" she whispered, her voice thick with tears. "Why wouldn't you let me close?"

He hesitated. "Because I knew if I let you close, I'd never let you go. And I couldn't have that. I'm sorry I . . . woke you, Jilly. Good night."

For a long time after he'd hung up, she cradled the receiver to her cheek, his words ricocheting through her head. Finally, when her fingers grew numb, she replaced the receiver and curled up under the covers.

Sleep took a long time coming.

❖────────────❖

Their short conversation changed them both, and for the next two weeks she and Jack skirted carefully around each other. They attended the welcome party, participated in two photo sessions, were featured on an early-morning KTBC talk show, and even helped host a *Save the Whales* charity event, all while managing to interact on a strictly professional level.

They'd taken pains not to tread on any too-personal ground and were careful that their bodies not brush, that their eyes not meet.

But even so, Jill had felt the awareness between them. His words, *I still want you . . . I want to make love with you,* hung heavily in the air between them, mocking her attempts at indifference and cool professionalism.

Jill drew a deep breath. Tonight she feared she wasn't up to the charade. Tonight she and Jack would share a limousine, they would sit together in a dark theater watching the premiere of the new Steven Spielberg film, they would attend the star-studded party afterward, drink champagne, talk, maybe dance.

With all that how could she keep the evening on a professional level? How could she keep her gaze from straying to his, her heart from thundering when he looked at her? And how could she keep from reacting if he touched her arm or the small of her back when he helped her from the limo?

She brought her hands to her burning cheeks. Did she really want to resist him?

Yes.

And no.

Jill gazed at herself in her full-length bedroom mirror. The woman who gazed back at her little resembled the one she was accustomed to seeing. Her cheeks were flushed, her eyes sparkled; she looked both excited and terrified.

She closed her eyes and took a deep, calming breath. Jack's honesty that night on the phone had moved her. He'd shared something of himself with her. He'd dug into his own heart, then offered what he'd found to her. It had taken a special kind of courage for him to do so.

Jack had changed. Maturity had taken the place of recklessness, self-confidence had replaced arrogance. She'd had an inkling of that at their first meeting when he'd tried to apologize to her for the past, but she hadn't seen it so clearly until the other night.

Jack had become the kind of man she had always dreamed of. If only he dreamed of a woman like her. If only he dreamed of a family and a love to last a lifetime.

In that way he hadn't changed.

Rebecca raced into the room, skidding to a stop when she saw her mother. Her eyes widened. "You look beautiful, Mommy." She wrinkled her nose. "Smell good too."

Jill smiled at her daughter. "Thank you, baby. Want to keep me company while I finish up?"

"Okay." Rebecca climbed onto the bed. "Margaret says I'm not supposed to bother you, 'else you'll be late."

"She did, did she?" Jill crossed to the dresser, picked up her earrings, and clipped them on. Margaret had been sitting for Rebecca since she was three months old and adored her. She also knew the two of them and their habits very well. "And what did you tell her?" Jill turned to face her daughter once more.

"I said I wouldn't."

"Good," she said sternly. "You know the rules. When I'm gone, Margaret's in charge and you have to li—"

The buzzer sounded, and Jill's stomach dropped to her toes. *Jack. He was early.*

"Let me!" Rebecca slid off the bed and galloped toward the door. "I'll go!"

Jill watched her daughter, then sucking in a shaky breath, returned her gaze to her reflection. Her dress was unrelieved black, made of antique lace, high-necked and old-fashioned. The sheath skimmed her body, stopping just above her knees. She'd pulled her hair up and back, anchoring it with a comb that had been her grandmother's. At her ears dangled black Austrian crystal earrings that had also belonged to her Grandmother Lansing.

Jill pressed a hand to her stomach. She'd been too nervous to eat all day. She'd alternated between wanting to hightail it out of town and daydreaming about the evening's possibilities. Not because of the industry bigwigs who would be in attendance, not because of the stars or the paparazzi or the opportunity to further her career.

Because of Jack.

Because she was falling in love with him. Again.

She spun away from her reflection. Crossing to the bed, she sank onto a corner, her arms curled around her middle. She couldn't be falling in love with him. She was older and wiser; she knew what she needed to be happy, and Jack wasn't it.

He would never love her.

He would never be a father for Rebecca.

But how could she have a future if she couldn't stop

loving Jack? She'd made that mistake once before—and others had been hurt. Badly hurt.

She made a sound of pain and covered her face in her hands. What was she going to do? How was she going to get through this?

"Mommy! Look!" Rebecca raced back into the room, waving a stuffed toy and almost tripping on the hem of her nightgown. "Look what Jack brought me."

Rebecca stopped in front of her, and Jill took the stuffed bear from her outstretched hands. The bear wore a pink tutu, toe shoes, and a precious expression. It was the perfect bear for a little girl, for her little girl. How had he known Rebecca was crazy about bears?

She rubbed her fingers over the bear's fuzzy head. "That was awfully nice of Jack. You did remember to say thank you?"

"Oops." Rebecca grabbed the bear and raced out of the room.

Jill smiled and shook her head, her heart beating slowly and heavily against the wall of her chest. Jack's gesture both surprised and touched her. Why had Jack brought Becky that sweet, silly little bear? He certainly hadn't needed to bring her daughter anything; she almost wished he hadn't. How was she going to remain cool and distant when every time she looked at him, she remembered his thoughtfulness and her daughter's excitement?

Saying a silent prayer for a level head, she stood, collected her purse and wrap, and headed down to meet him.

She found him in the living room, squatted next to Rebecca, his head bent as he listened raptly to one of her stories. She moved her gaze over him, taking in the black tuxedo and Mickey Mouse cummerbund and tie. She smiled at his choice even as she acknowledged that he looked wonderful.

As if becoming aware of her scrutiny, he looked up. "Hi."

She suddenly felt sixteen and foolish. "Hi."

He moved his gaze slowly over her. "You look sensational."

She saw frank male appreciation in his eyes. Her pulse fluttered, and she brought a hand nervously to her throat, then dropped it. "Thanks. I wondered if . . . I mean, I . . . Thanks."

He smiled and stood. "Rebecca was just telling me about her other bears."

Jill swallowed. "They're her favorite toys. Thank you for this one. That was very sweet of you."

He grinned, then ruffled Rebecca's hair. "I was happy to do it. Ready?"

Jill nodded and after giving the baby-sitter last minute instructions and hugging and kissing Rebecca, she and Jack headed out into the black velvet night. The cool air stung her cheeks, and Jill lifted her face to the stars. "It's a beautiful night."

"Yes," he murmured thickly. "Beautiful."

She met his eyes and blushed. He smiled at her obvious embarrassment and held out his arm. "Our carriage awaits. Shall we?"

She hesitated a moment, then slipped her hand into the crook of his arm. He covered her hand with his and tucked it against his side.

Keep this in perspective, she told herself. He was simply playing the gallant, attentive escort. But it was difficult to keep a clear head when her heart was pounding and her breath short, when his every touch or glance sent her pulse racing.

She shuddered, and he looked at her. "Are you cold?"

"I'm fine." She forced a smile. "Really."

They reached the limousine. The driver stood waiting, and as they approached, he nodded and opened the passenger door for them. Jill stepped inside the richly appointed vehicle. The interior of the car smelled of fine leather, and Jill eased onto the cushioned seat, liking the way it hugged her body.

Jack followed her in, sitting directly across from her. He opened a split of champagne and poured her a glass. Their fingers brushed as he handed it to her. Jill felt the touch like a brand and jerked her hand away, spilling some of the champagne. "Damn."

"Let me." He reached across with a napkin and patted the small puddle of liquid in her lap. "It'll be dry by the time we get to the theater."

She forced a smile. "Thanks."

He held up his glass, his eyes on hers. "To *Reel Reviews.*"

She tapped her glass against his and sipped. The champagne was cool, fine and dry; the bubbles tickled her nose and the back of her throat.

"Nervous?"

"Of course not. I'm just—" What? she wondered. Giddy at the sight of him? So sensitized to the sight, feel, and scent of him that she felt about to jump out of her skin? So hungry to touch him that she trembled?

Telling him the truth wasn't even an option.

She cleared her throat. "I feel a little silly going to a movie premiere like I'm some sort of celebrity."

"You are some sort of celebrity," he said dryly. "See?" The limo drew to a stop alongside a bus. From its side their own images looked back at them.

In the ad Jack faced the camera head-on, his mouth curved into the sexy, almost arrogant smile that so often sent her blood pressure skyrocketing. She stood beside him, head cocked, her gaze on him, her expression exasperated. The tag line read, *Jack and Jill . . . will they or won't they?*

She made a sound of surprise. And dismay. "I didn't expect to see them so soon. When did they go up?"

"Today I think. I saw one for the first time this afternoon."

The limousine started moving again, and she let out a relieved breath.

"Weird, isn't it?"

"Very. It's going to take some getting used to, seeing myself everywhere I go. And on such a grand scale."

He angled his body to get a last glance at the bus sign. "What do you think of the tag line?"

"Dana warned me that the campaign was going to play on the romance angle of the show, so at least I'm not surprised. How about you?"

Jack thought for a moment. "I understand it, what they're trying to do. And I think it'll be effective." He sat back in his seat and took a sip of his champagne. "We can always pretend it refers to whether we'll like a particular movie or not. And we might as well get used to it. By next week it's going to be everywhere."

Jill frowned. "I know. And it worries me."

"What?"

"I'm worried about Rebecca. About how she's going

to take this. I'm worried that seeing me . . . you know, everywhere, will confuse her."

Jack leaned toward her, grinning. "I think she's going to get a kick out of it. If I were a kid, I'd think it was pretty cool."

Jill smiled. "You're probably right. I worry too much sometimes."

"It's understandable. Especially considering the circumstances."

Jack leaned back in his seat, and Jill gazed out the window. Silence fell between them, thick with awareness, heavy with their shared history and awkward present, with thoughts left unspoken.

Jack studied her. They hadn't really spoken since the night he'd called her. They'd worked side by side without any personal interaction, without . . . intimacy.

It had been the hardest thing he'd ever done.

He'd longed to share details of his day with her, had time and again longed to whisper humorous asides in her ear, had longed to see her laugh, to earn her smile.

He hadn't given in to any of those longings, just as he hadn't given in to the urge to lay his hand against the smooth, warm skin of her cheek or to brush his mouth softly against the sweetness of hers.

That was then. Tonight he felt devoid of self-control, of the kind of willpower needed to deny himself her. Tonight she looked infinitely touchable. Soft and feminine and in need of a hero.

The last moved him the most.

He tightened his fingers on the champagne flute's delicate stem. He couldn't be anybody's hero. Not ever. He would do well to remember that.

He cleared his throat. "You have any plans for Thanksgiving?"

She shook her head. "Rebecca will be with Peter, and my parents are overseas on business."

"I'm sorry. I know how much the holidays mean to you."

She drew in a quiet breath. "That's life, I guess. I'm used to it."

But he could tell by her expression that she was not used to it. That the thought of spending Thanksgiving alone hurt her.

He noticed for the first time a ragged tear in the leather seat back, frowned at it a moment, then met her gaze once more. "Why did you divorce . . . him?"

"I didn't. He divorced me," she said evenly.

Jack bit back a sound of surprise. *He'd asked her for a divorce? Did that mean she still loved the guy? That if he hadn't left her, she would still be married to him today?* The thought took his breath away.

"We never should have gotten married," she murmured. "I see that now. It was a big mistake."

"But if you hadn't, you wouldn't have Becky." The words, the thought, spilled off his tongue before he even realized it was there. He didn't like the way it made him feel, exposed and too involved. Way too involved.

Before she could comment, he leaned toward her, grinning wickedly. "I've got big plans for Thanksgiving."

"You do?"

"Yeah, I'm planning to wangle a dinner invitation out of some unsuspecting friends."

She laughed. "Same old classy Jack."

"Yeah, you know me." He thought back five years

and smiled. "Remember the Thanksgiving we spent together?"

He saw her stiffen, but he didn't try to take the question back or change the subject. He wanted to remember that day, even though many times over the past five years he'd cursed not being able to forget it. That day had been special. The most special.

He leaned across the seat and caught her hand, curving his fingers around hers. "Do you remember, Jilly?"

She gazed at their joined hands, then lifted her eyes to his. "How could I forget, Jack? That was the night—" She shook her head. "I remember you laughed at the idea of a turkey with all the trimmings just for us. You thought my domestic tendencies were pretty silly."

He frowned. "That's not true."

"No? The way I remember—" Again she shook her head. "Let's not dredge up the past, it doesn't do either of us any good."

He moved his thumb along the side of her hand, stroking, soothing. "That was the best Thanksgiving I ever had. I loved it, Jilly."

She met his eyes, and his heart turned over. "The next year I tried to re-create it." He laughed softly. "My turkey was burned on the outside and raw on the inside. I hadn't gotten around to completely thawing it, so I turned up the oven so that it would cook faster."

She smiled. "Sounds tasty."

He laughed again and slipped his fingers in between hers. "Oh, yeah. I ended up going out for a bucket of the Colonel's special recipe. My sister, Sue, was visiting, and believe me, she was impressed. She called me classy too."

Jill laughed. "You just can't help yourself."

He gazed at their joined hands for a moment, then brought them to his mouth. He felt her fingers tremble in his. "You're right, Jilly. I can't help myself."

"Jack, don't."

"I know." He brushed his mouth across her knuckles, then released her hand. "But there are times I just . . . forget."

The limo slowed to a crawl, and Jack peered out the window. Up ahead he saw one of Hollywood's most famous sights, Mann's Chinese Theater. Fans eager to see the parade of celebrities jammed the sidewalk in every direction and lined the walkway to the theater. The media were in attendance as well; as he watched, strobes flashed and the crowd seemed to go crazy.

"We're almost there," he murmured. "And none too early; it looks like the headliners just arrived."

She followed his gaze, then groaned and leaned her head against the seat back. "I wish we could skip this. I'm not the lights-and-cameras type."

"We could. Play hooky, I mean."

"You wouldn't!"

"Want to bet on it?" He held out a hand. She stared at it, her expression a mixture of disbelief and wishful thinking.

"Dana would have our heads."

He laughed. "That's the risk you take when you cut class. Sometimes you get caught."

She laughed and shook her head. "And go to the principal's office? No way. Dana's tougher than she looks."

Their limo pulled to a stop, and the driver came around and opened the door for them. "Let's do it," Jack said.

As they stepped out of the limousine, lights flashed, the crowd cheered, and reporters rushed forward. Interest immediately waned as the crowd realized they weren't stars. Undaunted and amused, Jack smiled and waved.

Jill leaned toward him. "Enjoying this, aren't you?"

He curved his arm around her. "Just playing for the crowd, that's all."

"It's Jack and Jill," a girl near the barrier called out. "From *Reel Reviews*. He's so cute!" Jack threw her a kiss, and she squealed in response.

Moments later they entered the theater. Jack bent his head to hers. "That wasn't so bad, was it?"

She angled her face up to his. "Easy for you to say, I didn't get called cute."

He leaned his face a fraction closer. Her breath stirred against his mouth; their lips hovered only inches apart. Hunger tightened in his gut.

He saw an answering arousal come into her eyes, an answering heat. If he dipped his head, he knew, she would meet him halfway. He cursed their very public surroundings.

He straightened. "Come on, let's go to our seats."

Famous faces dotted the audience, many of them with their kids in tow. He saw Kevin Costner and Susan Sarandon, Michelle Pfeiffer and Whoopi Goldberg. He recognized studio executives and world-class directors, a *New York Times* best-selling author, and daytime TV's most popular talk-show host.

He only had eyes for Jill. She sat ramrod straight next to him, her hands clasped in her lap, her gaze fixed firmly on the blank screen. He sensed a little-girl expectation in her, an excitement born of a real love for the movies.

He smiled. She was special. Exquisitely so. As they had in the limo, memories swamped him. Of that Thanksgiving night, of making love, their mouths still sweet and sticky from pumpkin pie and whipped cream, of her insistence that they put up the Christmas tree the next day, of their making love under its twinkling lights, that night and every night until they took the tree down the day after New Year's.

She'd made him feel young and carefree. She'd made him laugh. She'd made him feel . . . loved. His throat closed over the thought, and he fought to clear it. He hadn't felt any of those things since.

The lights dimmed. The opening credits rolled, the movie's theme song with them. Still he gazed at her, the scent of her perfume, at once earthy and innocent, filling his head, his senses.

She caught him staring at her and searched his expression. "What?"

He shook his head, a smile pulling at the corners of his mouth. "I can't seem to stop looking at you."

Even in the darkened theater he saw her blush. She looked away, then back, obviously embarrassed. "Stop anyway."

"I'll try."

"Thank you."

He didn't. He couldn't.

After a moment she turned her head again. "Jack," she whispered, "the movie's started."

"Has it?"

She drew her eyebrows together. "Stop it. Please."

He grinned, liking her fluster. "Yes, ma'am."

He managed to keep his word and turned his gaze toward the screen. The film, in classic Spielberg fashion, told a story about the magic and fantasy of childhood brought to life for adults. The main protagonist was a young boy in search of his father. He's aided in his search by his three favorite stuffed toys, all of which he had brought to life by wishing, with all his heart, that it would happen.

At the film's climax he heard Jill sniffle, and he reached across and squeezed her hand, his own heart in his throat, emotion choking him. As if sensing his feelings, she curved her fingers around his. They sat that way until the closing credits rolled and the house lights came up.

She released his hand and surreptitiously wiped at her eyes. The movie had tugged at his own heartstrings, and he'd been unable to stop thinking about his own childhood, his own relationship with his father. He shook his melancholy off and grinned at her. "Are you crying, Ms. Lansing?"

She sniffed and inched her chin up. "Of course not. I'm much too world-weary and jaded for that."

"Right." He stood. "Better not let anyone see you, or they won't have to tune in to the show to know your review."

She followed him to his feet. "Are you so sure? Just because I cry doesn't mean I think a movie's without flaws."

He laughed. "I think I know you well enough to write your review."

"Arrogant pig."

He laughed again, and they started up the aisle.

The lobby was a mob scene. A reporter from *Enter-*

tainment Tonight recognized Jack from his work in *People*, and approached them to get their reactions to the movie. They both sidestepped the question by indicating that the curious should tune into *Reel Reviews*.

After being stopped, jostled, and bumped into a couple of dozen times, Jack muttered, "Let's get out of here. I know this great little cantina that serves nachos all night and makes the best margaritas you ever tasted."

"What about the party?"

"I vote we skip it." He grinned wickedly. "I'm in the mood for Mexican under the stars."

Jill returned his grin. "Dana pulled some pretty powerful strings to get those invitations."

"She'd understand. We're talking world-class margaritas here."

With a laugh Jill agreed.

SIX

The open-air cantina did indeed serve the best margaritas Jill had ever tasted. Although in truth she couldn't testify to whether the margaritas alone tasted so good or whether drinking them with Jack enhanced their flavor.

She sipped the sweet, frozen drink, the salt on the glass's rim stinging her tongue, her gaze on Jack. He leaned back in his chair, arms folded across his chest as he spoke to the restaurant's owner. He'd removed his tie, jacket, and cummerbund in the limo, had rolled his shirt sleeves up to his elbows, and had loosened his collar. He looked relaxed, confident, and potently male.

She smiled to herself and took another sip of the frozen concoction. What was it about a man in formal attire that she found so sexy? Her lips curved up. Not just wearing dress clothes, but defying them?

Not any man, she thought. *This man. Jack.*

Her man.

Cheeks burning, she took another sip. Those kinds of thoughts would land her in trouble. Those kinds of thoughts would have her doing and saying things she would regret forever. Why couldn't she remember that?

The restaurateur walked away, and Jack turned his eyes on her. He arched an eyebrow. "You look like the proverbial cat that swallowed the canary."

"Do I?"

"Mmm." He moved his gaze slowly over her. "Satisfied but still hungry."

The heat in her cheeks became fire. "It must be the tequila." She tipped her head back, taking in the black sky and bright stars. Strung with tiny white lights, the outdoor café melded with the star-dotted sky. She breathed deeply. The nearly empty patio, the piped-in music, and the warm, scented breeze added to the sensation of being in another world, a place created just for them.

More dangerous thoughts.

Jack leaned toward her. "What are you thinking?"

She returned her gaze to his, fighting the urge to tell him exactly what she was thinking, fighting the urge to flirt openly and shamelessly with him. "I was wondering how you found this place. It's a bit off the beaten path."

He smiled. "Trying to find another place actually. A French bistro someone told me about. Hopelessly lost and starving, I stopped here."

"Still have an aversion to maps, I see," she teased.

He laughed. "If I'd used a map, I never would have found this place."

"True." She touched her forefinger to the glass's salty rim, then brought it to her mouth and sucked the salt off. Enjoying its tang, she did it again. Then again.

"One more time, Jilly, and I won't be responsible for my actions."

She stopped, surprised, her finger halfway to her mouth. Jack's eyes were fixed on her mouth, dark with awareness. Heat flooded her, and she dropped her hand to her lap.

"Thank you," he said, his voice unnaturally thick.

"You're welcome."

He smiled. "You were always able to do that, you know."

She looked away, then back. "What?"

"Drive me crazy without even trying."

Her world rocked on its axis. She searched for something to say. Something neutral, something that wouldn't add to awareness already consuming her.

She took a deep breath. "This reminds me of that little Mexican place we used to go to. What was it called?"

"Dos Guys."

She laughed. "That's right. I haven't been there in years."

"Nobody has." He trailed his finger down the side of his sweating glass. "They went out of business."

"No? The food was so good."

"The couple who owned it split up and—" He lifted his shoulders. "It was never the same."

Never the same, she thought. The way she'd been after she and Jack had split up. She forced the melancholy thought away.

"Remember the first time we went there?"

She nodded, swallowing past the lump that formed in her throat. "The night we met."

"We were introduced at the *Working Girl* premiere," he murmured. "Remember?"

"Mmm. We despised each other on sight." Her lips

curved up. "You goaded me into agreeing to go someplace to discuss the movie. I couldn't believe you wanted to pan it."

"I couldn't believe you loved it."

"We argued for hours." She laughed softly. "You never did sway me."

"Sure I did." He reached across the table and covered her hand with his. Lightly he trailed his fingers over hers, dipping them in and out of the junctures between. "I quite clearly remember swaying you."

"You didn't!" She laughed and started to draw her hand away. He closed his fingers around hers and brought her hand to his mouth. He trailed his lips across its back. She shuddered at the sensation, goose bumps racing up her arms.

"I did." He lifted his lips in a wicked smile. "About six hours later. In bed."

Heat flew to her cheeks even as her pulse began to thrum. She remembered being shocked by her own behavior. Stunned, even. She'd never done that before, had never acted so brazen, so wanton. She remembered being both tiger and kitten with him. Jack had always brought out everything in her, aspects of herself she hadn't even known existed.

She arched her eyebrows in mock disbelief, "We certainly did not make love the first day we met."

"Call it the second, then," he said, self-satisfaction gleaming in his eyes. "It was almost morning."

Embarrassed, she looked away. It was true. Their affair had been explosive, their reactions to each other immediate and overpowering. She had become a woman she hadn't recognized.

"Don't, Jilly," he murmured, caressing her fingers.

"Don't be ashamed. I'm a man, but it wasn't any different for me. You made me weak, just looking at you, with nothing more than a single, innocent touch." He lowered his voice. "You still do."

He opened her hand and kissed her palm. The blood rushed dizzyingly to her head. Places that should have been strong became weak and aching; places that had already ached for him began to throb.

"It wasn't all physical," he murmured, holding her with his hot gaze. "Remember the way we talked?"

She wetted her lips. "We argued."

"Discussed." Still holding her hand, he stood. He held out his other hand. "Dance with me, Jilly."

She shook her head. "No one else is dancing."

"No one else is here."

She looked around the empty patio. Their limo driver sat at the bar, watching a late-night talk show, a cup of coffee in front of him. The restaurant's owner sat at a table just inside the cantina, deep in conversation with the establishment's only other patron.

She looked helplessly at Jack. "But—"

"Come on, Jilly." He lowered his voice to a seductive murmur. "Dance with me."

She placed her trembling hand in his, and he drew her to her feet. They made their way to a clearing between the tables, and Jack took her into his arms.

Jill squeezed her eyes shut and breathed deeply through her nose, growing intoxicated on the scent of the night, the feel of Jack's breath stirring against her cheek, the brush of his body against hers. If she died and went to heaven, heaven would surely be an eternity in his arms.

Jill relaxed against him as they swayed to the dreamy

music, letting him lead her. They moved as one, intuitively knowing the other's next step. They always had—when they danced or kissed . . . when they made love. It had been that way from the very first.

She made a small sound of pleasure, deep in her throat, and he pressed her closer. Their bodies fit as if they'd been fashioned specially for each other. She lifted her lips in a small, contented smile. No one had ever fit her the way he had. It was as if their internal blueprints were exact but opposite matches—like a photograph and its negative. When put together, they made a perfect picture.

She'd never understood it.

And tonight she hadn't the desire—or the will—to fight it.

"I've missed you, Jilly," he murmured, toying with the wisps of hair at her nape that had come loose of her comb.

She lifted her face to his. "Have you, Jack?"

"God, yes." He lowered his head and trailed his mouth across the arch of her brow, then pressed his lips against her hair. "Nobody's ever made me feel the way you do."

"I know." She slid her hands up his chest to his shoulders. Still moving to the music, she laced them behind his neck. "Me either."

"What happened to us?" He cupped her face in his hands and gazed deeply into her eyes. "This feels so good . . . so right. How did we let each other slip away?"

He brought his mouth to hers, softly, brushing his lips against hers, tasting, exploring, reinventing him and her together. Sensation after sensation washed over her in warm, tingling waves. She curled her fingers around his shoulders.

Jack's kiss. She remembered everything about it, about being with him. His taste. His scent. The way he tilted his head when he took her mouth; the sound he made as he loved her.

The memories were good. Very good. She stood on tiptoe and pressed herself more fully to him. Deepening their kiss. She felt his arousal as clearly as her own, and she thrilled in it, in knowing that the past five years had not weakened or dissipated his response to her.

With a groan Jack dragged his mouth away from hers, his breathing fast, labored with passion. He met her eyes. She saw his arousal . . . and uncertainty. A hesitation she never would have associated with Jack. She'd always known he desired her, and that had pleased her, but the uncertainty, the hint of vulnerability she saw in him now touched her. Deeply.

"What happened?" he repeated, searching her expression, burying his fingers in her hair, tumbling it loose of its restraint. The antique comb clattered against the tile patio floor. "How did we go from everything to nothing in a matter of moments?"

She opened her mouth to answer, but before she could, he captured her lips again with a muffled oath. Like a drowning man, he devoured her mouth. She answered in kind, clinging to him, parting her lips, taking everything he would give her.

And wishing with all her heart for what he would never give her.

She pushed that thought from her mind, and the feeling of hopelessness that came with it. For now she would think only of tonight and this moment. Tomorrow would take care of itself.

He tightened his fingers in her hair; she pressed herself closer to him. He tasted of the tequila and lime; he smelled of the night and her own perfume. She closed her eyes again, focusing on every detail, wanting to bury each one so deeply in her memory that she would never forget even a nuance of tonight.

"Jill . . . Jill . . ." He tore his mouth from hers and brought it to her ear, pressing a kiss to the pulse that beat just below. "I couldn't believe it when you left me," he murmured. He moved his mouth to the other ear. "I just . . . couldn't . . . believe when you . . . How could you have married him?"

She opened her eyes, his words intruding rudely on her soft, warm world. *I couldn't believe it when you left me. . . . How could you have married him?*

She drew in a deep, shaking breath. He said those words as if he had been the victim, she the villain. He said them as if she had walked out coldly and without a backward glance.

He had pushed her out of his life; he had left her no choice but to leave. No choice but to go on with her life.

It had broken her heart.

She moved her hands from his shoulders to his chest, adrenaline pumping through her, bringing anger with it. Beneath her palm his heart thundered. She flattened her hands and pushed. Jack relaxed his hold, and she tipped her head back and met his eyes, still clouded with passion. "Why couldn't you believe it?" she asked softly but with an unmistakable edge. "Because I was so stupidly, so head-over-heels in love with you?"

She saw reality race into his eyes, saw his arousal

begin to dim, replaced by confusion. Then disbelief. He frowned and shook his head. "I didn't mean that."

"Then what did you mean? Exactly?"

He dropped his arms. "That you didn't give me any warning. You just . . . moved out. Less than six months later I hear you're married to somebody else."

"What did you expect? If you were me, what would you have done? You'd given me my walking papers." She hugged herself, suddenly cold. "You told me you didn't love me. That you didn't want to marry me. There was no future in you and me."

"That's not true. I was willing to try to make it work. I told you that before I left. You took off instead." He flexed his fingers. "You didn't even have the decency to tell me about the baby."

"Decency?" She swung away from him, tears choking her. "You were furious when I told you I thought I was pregnant. You accused me of trying to trap you into marrying me."

"I was young and a hothead. You caught me totally off guard." He lowered his voice. "I know you didn't try to trap me, Jilly. It's not in you to be dishonest."

She faced him defiantly. "Easy to say now, isn't it?"

"It's all got to be your way, doesn't it?" He took a step back from her. "No compromise, nobody else's opinion matters. That's why you walked, it's why you didn't even bother to call me about the pregnancy. I had a right to know."

"Did you?" She curved her arms around herself. "You made it clear you weren't interested in becoming a father. In fact you made all your feelings perfectly clear."

"So you turned right around and found somebody else, somebody who would do it your way."

Blood rushed to her cheeks, fury with it. "What would you know about compromise, Jack? What would you know about settling, or conceding a point? My God, you're so inflexible, you haven't spoken to your father in six years."

Her barb struck its mark. Jack's mouth tightened with pain, and she wished she could take back her words. She couldn't, she knew.

"Thank you, Jilly. That was sweet of you." His expression was as sarcastic as his tone. "Feel better now that you're back in control?"

"I'm leaving."

"Of course you are. Hard to break those old habits, isn't it?"

"Damn you." She spun away from him and marched toward the bar. Jack followed. The limo driver jumped up, leaving his plate of nachos behind. He rushed to the vehicle and swung the door open for her. Before she could slip inside, Jack caught up with her. He grabbed her elbow and turned her to face him.

"Earlier I asked what had happened to us. Now I remember. This happened to us."

"What?" she shot back. "*My* walking out? *My* unwillingness to bend, to settle for less?"

"No," Jack said softly. "*Our* unwillingness to bend. I'll take some of the responsibility, Jill. But not all of it. You played a part in our breakup."

She stared at him a moment, her heart thundering, then she shook her head slowly. "No. You left me nothing to compromise on. I wanted a family, Jack." She pressed a hand to her chest. "I wanted children. And you wanted neither. What was I supposed to do, give up my dreams, wait forever for something that would never happen?"

"That last day, before I left for Cannes, I told you I was willing to try to work things out, to compromise. We had everything, Jill, then you—"

"No." She shook her head again and freed her arm from his grasp. "We could have had everything. But we didn't. Because you were never willing to give everything. You were never willing to give yourself."

He made a sound of frustration and dragged a hand through his hair. "Once again you've left me in a no-win situation. What do you want me to say?"

"Nothing. There's nothing to say."

Neither of them moved. She saw vulnerability come into his eyes, a need she'd never seen in him before. And then it was gone, replaced by steely determination and cool distance. She told herself she'd imagined it.

She took a step into the car. He murmured her name, stopping her. She met his eyes.

He hesitated, then shook his head. "Go on. The driver's waiting."

She slid into the car. He followed her. This time they shared neither champagne nor soft laughter. This time they faced each other, but avoided each other's eyes, didn't speak or smile.

The car began to move, the miles to pass. And with each mile the quiet ate at her more. The evening had begun so wonderfully. They'd talked and laughed. The moments in his arms had been exquisite.

How could she have kidded herself? How could she have let down her guard and allowed herself to forget, even if only for those perfect moments, how much Jack had hurt her?

She brought her hand to her mouth, which was still tingling from his kiss. Realizing what she was doing—and what he would think—she dropped it to her lap. Five years ago she had gone on without him. Without his touch, his kiss, the magic that had been her and Jack together. And in the ensuing years her memory of how wonderful it had been with him had dimmed.

Now she'd been reminded. Now her memory rang with him. How would she go on this time? How would she forget?

Tomorrow had come so much sooner than she'd expected.

The limo drew to a stop in front of her complex. The driver came around and opened her door. She started to climb out, tears stinging her eyes. Once again Jack caught her hand, stopping her. She met his eyes.

"I went through hell that week in Cannes, thinking of you, and me, and the baby I thought was growing inside you. Worrying about what to do, what was best for all of us. I came home two days early, with a ring and a speech I'd practiced until I knew it by heart. But you were gone."

She sucked in a sharp breath, her world tilting on its axis. *He'd meant to propose. He'd been willing to marry her. But she'd already been gone.*

"You weren't the only one hurt, Jilly." He dropped her hand. "Think about that next time you want to wholesale blame me for the past."

For one long moment she gazed at him, the tears in her eyes threatening to spill over, words with them. Apologies and pleas, regrets.

She shook her head. Nothing could change the past.

Nothing could erase the pain they'd inflicted on each other; the scars ran too deep.

Without a word she climbed out of the car, and crossed to her front gate. Jack didn't make a move to walk her to the door, but she didn't expect him to. Heart aching, she turned and watched the limo drive away.

A week later Jack's words still taunted her. She frowned into her dressing-room mirror, a jar of cold cream in her hands. Had Jack been hurt when he'd returned home to find her gone, to find that there wasn't, and had never been, a baby?

She'd never thought so, had always looked at herself as the wounded party. She'd loved him; he hadn't loved her. Black and white, very simple. Thinking that had made it easier to hate him, easier to give up on him and go on.

Had she played more of a role in her and Jack's breakup than she'd ever admitted?

Now she wondered. Now she was unable to put Jack, and their past, from her mind. She'd been unable to sleep or concentrate, her appetite had all but disappeared, and she'd found herself mulling over her and Jack, the past and the present, at all hours of the day and night.

With a sigh she dipped her fingers into the cream and spread it over her face and neck. Using tissues, she removed the heavy makeup, then cleansed her skin with a damp washcloth.

Jack had been willing to marry her. He said he'd returned from Cannes prepared to do just that. But would it have changed anything?

No. He hadn't wanted to marry her, he hadn't loved her. He'd come to that decision only out of a sense of obligation and guilt.

But still he had been ready to compromise, to bend. She hadn't. She frowned at her reflection. Maybe he was right. Maybe she always had to have her way, always had to call the shots and be in control. She didn't like to think so; she didn't find those character traits very appealing.

She fisted her fingers, thinking of her loveless childhood. She'd spent so much time alone, so much time with people paid to care for her. Her parents had been busy people. She had been an accident; her parents had never planned on children. And they'd vowed to go on with their lives and careers as if nothing had changed.

And they had. She'd had to fight for every scrap of attention she'd gotten from them, had learned to depend on herself, had learned the importance of being strong-willed and single-minded.

So maybe Jack was right. Maybe she had walked out because of her unwillingness to compromise. But would anything have changed if she had stayed? She shook her head. She thought not. The past couldn't be changed; it was done with. Only the future remained, and at this moment it was more disturbing than the past.

Rebecca.

Jill brought a hand to her temple and massaged at the headache that hammered there. The publicity blitz was in full swing. Everywhere she went, she saw pictures of her and Jack—on billboards and the sides of buses, the "People" section of the *L.A. Times.* And the tag line, *Jack and Jill . . . Will they or won't they?* seemed to mock her from all directions.

Rebecca had seemed to enjoy seeing pictures of her mother everywhere they went, and her teachers at pre-school had assured her they'd noticed no change in Rebecca's behavior or emotional state.

Peter, on the other hand, was not handling it well at all. He'd called the other night furious and had coldly informed her that she was endangering their daughter's emotional health. Rebecca, he'd said, had been tense, unhappy, and near tears since she'd arrived there. He'd insinuated that he was going to use this against her at the custody hearing.

His call had frightened her. Badly. She'd called her lawyer immediately, and he'd assured her that Peter's threats were hogwash. But her fears hadn't been allayed. Peter, she knew, would use any means available to win custody of Rebecca.

Jill shuddered. Short of pulling out of the show—and breaking her contract—she didn't see how she could put an end to the publicity. The show had caught fire, although she still couldn't quite fathom its popularity. The letters and calls had continued to pour in, and they were quickly becoming one of California's most popular local shows.

She picked up her brush and ran it through her hair. For whatever reason, she and Jack had caught the imagination of the viewing public. The viewers either loved or despised one or the other of them; they were fixated on the idea that she and Jack should become lovers. They thought they were perfect for each other.

So had she. Once.

Jill tossed down the brush and stood, disgusted with herself and her own thoughts. The publicity was part of her job. As was making appearances with Jack and putting up a good front for the public. She crossed to the door and stepped out into the hallway. She would continue to participate, and happily, as long as doing so didn't hurt Rebecca or her chances of winning custody of her.

"Hey, Jilly."

She blinked, seeing Jack for the first time. He was coming down the hallway in her direction, hands shoved into his front pockets, a newspaper tucked under his arm. "Hey to you too." She searched his expression. "I thought you left."

"I had. I saw this and came back." He held out the newspaper. "We made the 'People' section again."

She looked at the paper Jack had opened and folded to the piece in question. A picture of the two of them, taken at the opening of a new mall theater complex, stared back at her. She caught her bottom lip between her teeth. They'd attended the opening for publicity purposes, and Jack had hammed it up, kneeling in front of her, taking her hand and pretending to be the smitten, rejected lover.

Heat stung her cheeks. People had eaten it up. Dana and the powers-that-be at the station had been pleased. Jack had seemed to have a great time, seemed to have been born for the limelight.

It had made her feel exposed and vulnerable. She couldn't control her physical or emotional reactions to Jack, and she hated feeling as if all the California viewers were getting a peek into her heart.

Of course he didn't mind, because he had no feelings to expose. He had never been in love with her.

"Better read the blurb."

She lifted her eyes to Jack's, then lowered them to the blurb.

The paper had found out that she and Jack had once been lovers. Someone had told them.

Her heart sank. Had Peter seen this? she wondered, a sense of dread settling over her. If he had, he would be beyond furious. His pride would be stung. She knew him well enough to know that. And to know that, if he could, he would use it against her. He hated Jack. He'd been almost insanely jealous of him when they'd been married, refusing to listen to her avowals that she was over the other man.

But would it add fuel to his "case" against her?

"Are you okay?"

She shrugged. "Sure."

She didn't fool him. He caught her hands and searched her expression. She worked to hide how upset she was, how frightened. She could see by his face that she'd failed miserably.

"It's not that big a deal," he said softly. "So what if people know that once upon a time we were lovers? It happens all the time."

"This isn't about me and my feelings. It's—" She swallowed hard, battling the tears that choked her, that threatened to spill over. She shook her head. "Never mind. I've got to go."

She tried to slip her hands from his, but he tightened his grip. "Talk to me, Jill. This is about more than a blurb in the paper. What is it?"

She hesitated. "It's Peter. He called the other night, furious about all the publicity. He says it's hurting Rebecca and that . . . he's going to use it against me."

Jack swore. "That bastard. The only thing that's going to hurt Rebecca is his insistence on fighting you for custody."

"My lawyer says he doesn't think my being in the limelight is going to sway the judge's opinion, but I can't help worrying." She lifted her gaze to his once more. "What if it does? I'm scared, Jack."

Swearing again, softly this time, he eased her against his chest. "I know, baby. But it's going to be okay."

"I wish I could be sure. I wish I didn't know Peter as well as I do."

He stroked her hair. "I could talk to him. Maybe he would—"

"No!" She lifted her face to his. "Don't go near Peter. I don't know what he might do if you two ever came face-to-face."

Jack frowned. "Why? He doesn't even know me."

"Never mind." She shook her head. "Just promise me you won't contact him. Please."

Jack curved his fingers around her upper arms. "Not unless you tell me why."

She saw that he meant what he said and drew a deep, shuddering breath. "Peter blames you, my feelings for you, for the failure of our marriage."

"But that's crazy. You and I were finished before you met him. I hadn't spoken to you until a few weeks ago."

"He doesn't believe that. He was always jealous of you. He accused me of seeing you during our marriage." She clasped her hands together. "And when I proved to him that I'd been faithful, he accused me of still . . . loving you. That's why he divorced me."

Jack took a step back from her, his expression stunned.

She gazed at him a moment, then looked away. "And

this publicity . . . it's reinforcing what he believed all along. I'm so afraid he'll do something. Use it somehow."

"What can I do?"

"Nothing." She shook her head and drew a deep breath. "I've got to go, Rebecca's waiting."

She turned and hurried down the hall, achingly aware of Jack's silence and his troubled gaze on her back.

SEVEN

Sunlight tumbled through Jack's bedroom window, sending fingers of light spilling across the bed. Wakefulness pushed at the edges of his sleep, nudging at the world of dreams. Jack groaned and pulled the pillow over his face. The dream playing in his head was good, too good to abandon to the day. In it Jill was with him, naked, sitting on the edge of the bed and smiling at him. In it he was completely contented, a man at peace with the world.

Jack groaned again, fighting to hold on to the dream and the place that felt so warm and wonderful. It eluded him, and with a muttered oath he tossed off the pillow and sat up. Yawning, he stretched and scratched his chest, then cocked his head. The house resounded with quiet. It smelled as empty as it sounded. No scent of brewing coffee or burned toast. No slamming doors or cheerfully whistled tunes. No Jill on the edge of the bed, smiling at him as if he were the most wonderful thing in the world.

That had been a dream.

Another Thanksgiving spent alone.

Jack propped the pillows up behind him and leaned against them. Frowning, he dragged his hands through his hair and thought of the conversation he'd had with his sister, Sue, the other day. She had urged him to come home for Thanksgiving, she had tried to talk him into it.

"Come on, Jack," she had pleaded. "It's Thanksgiving. We could all be together."

Jack had kept his tone easy, even as tension had tightened at the back of his neck. "Sorry, Sue, but it's not going to happen."

"You could fly in for Thursday, fly out on Friday," she'd continued, only slightly daunted. "You wouldn't even miss a day's work. And it would make Mom so happy."

Guilt had spiraled through him. And longing so sharp, it took his breath. "Mom's coming out with Bonnie and the twins in a few weeks."

"That's not the same as having all of us there for the holiday meal."

"Leave it alone, baby sister."

She'd made a sound of frustration. "You're just like Dad, you know that, Jack? One selfish S.O.B."

Anger surged through him. "Then why are you calling me, Sue? If I'm such a selfish S.O.B., why do you want me around?"

For a moment his sister had said nothing, then she swore softly. "I didn't mean that. It's just that . . . you're my brother and I love you. We all do and . . . we'd like to have you around."

Jack closed his fingers around the phone cord, fighting the emotion that threatened to choke him. "I know, and I'd . . . like to be around too. But this thing with me and Dad, it's not going to go away. I can't . . . bend on this. I won't."

He had forced a laugh then; to his own ears it had sounded tight and humorless. "Besides, me and Dad glaring at each other wouldn't make for good digestion."

Jack shook his head and turned his gaze to his bedroom window and the bright day beyond. Since that conversation he had been plagued with thoughts of home and his past.

Home.

Jill.

His head filled with her, with memories of that magic Thanksgiving they'd spent together, with visions of the other night when they'd danced, with the image of her from his dream, sitting on the edge of his bed smiling at him.

He drew in a ragged breath, his chest tight, the memories clawing at him. Was Jill making a turkey this year, with all the trimmings, as she had when they lived together? He smiled, remembering her in her frilly apron, recalling the delicious aromas that had filled the house, recalling that she'd been up at dawn to start the pies, that they'd made love three times before the day had come to a close.

The night of the premiere he'd held her in his arms again, he'd kissed her. It had been as exciting, as incredible, as it had always been between them. Even more so.

How could she still affect him so strongly? After all the years that had passed, after all the water under their personal bridges?

He dragged his hands through his hair once more. He'd been unable to stop thinking of her, of what she'd told him the other day. Her words rang through his head, taunting him. *"Peter blamed you for our failed marriage. He divorced me because he believed I still loved you."*

Jack threw the covers aside, climbed out of bed, and stalked to the window. The cloudless blue sky seemed to mock him.

Was it true? Had she still loved him? He shook his head. He doubted it. Her ex-husband was an insecure and jealous fool. Peter had had a wonderful prize, but he'd been too blind to see it.

But so had he.

A knot of tension balled at the back of his neck, and he scowled at the blue-and-gold day. That was different. He wasn't a marrying man. Wasn't a man who looked for commitment and family ties. He'd chosen a different path long ago, the only path for him. He couldn't—he wouldn't—veer from it.

But that didn't mean he hadn't cared for Jill. That didn't mean he hadn't been torn apart when she'd walked out. He brought a hand to the back of his neck and worked the knotted muscles. She accused him of not having given anything of himself to their relationship. If that was true, why had it hurt so bad when it ended? If he hadn't had a stake in their relationship, why was he still, five years later, so consumed with it?

Forget it, he told himself. Let her think whatever she wanted of him. It was over. They were over.

He shook his head. Who was he trying to kid? If their relationship was over, he wouldn't be thinking about her morning, noon, and night. He wouldn't be dreaming about her. If it were over, kissing her wouldn't make him ache clear to his bones.

And he wouldn't be worried about her and the possibility of her losing custody of her daughter.

He swore and swung away from the window. Was losing Rebecca a real possibility? Was there a chance that *Reel Reviews* and the publicity surrounding the show could hurt Jill's chances in court?

Concern twisted in his gut. And guilt at the part he played in the situation, even if only indirectly.

This was crazy. Nuts. He dragged his hands through his hair. He'd allowed himself to be drawn into her life. Into Rebecca's. How had it happened? And so quickly? The last time he'd become involved with Jill, he'd almost forgotten his vows of freedom. He'd almost forgotten the lessons he'd learned living with his father.

He needed to check out of Jill's life, of this situation, immediately. He needed to put her and her daughter from his mind and go on with his life—the life he'd planned and worked for, the life that was just the way he wanted it.

Rebecca would be with her father today. Jill would be alone. And sad. She needed him.

And he needed her.

Jack frowned. As much as he hated to admit it, he didn't want to be alone today. No, it was more personal than that. He didn't want to be without Jill.

Ignoring all the reasons he should be smart and stay away, he headed to the bathroom to shower.

He made it to her place before noon. Judging by the parking area, the majority of her neighbors had headed elsewhere for the day. Her white Volvo was one of the few vehicles in the lot.

He rang her buzzer. She answered almost immediately, her voice thick and raspy. For one moment the sound of her voice stole his ability to think, to respond.

"Yes?" she repeated. "Is anyone there?"

"Jilly . . . it's me. Jack. Are you all right?"

For a second she said nothing. "I'm fine."

Silence stretched between them, potent with the things they both left unsaid. He cleared his throat. "I was hoping, I . . . I'd like to come up, Jilly."

Again she hesitated. He could almost hear her frown. "I don't think that's a good idea."

He flexed his fingers as disappointment and longing spiraled through him. "Jilly . . . it's Thanksgiving. I'm alone. So are you." He lifted his gaze to her windows. "And there's nobody else I want to be with."

She swore softly. "I'll buzz you in."

She did and he pushed through the iron gate, then crossed the courtyard to her front door. As he reached it, she swung it open.

She wore an apron similar to the one he remembered from all those years ago; under it she wore khaki shorts and a white T-shirt. He moved his gaze over her face. Her cheeks were pink, wisps of her hair had escaped its clip and tumbled against her cheek and the nape of her neck. A dusting of flour decorated her forehead and the side of her nose.

She'd been crying.

His heart tipped over. "Are you okay?"

"That's the second time you've asked me that." He saw her try to act nonchalant. "Do I look sick?"

"No." He lowered his voice and took a step toward her. "You look sad."

She turned away from him, heading back into the house. He followed her. As he stepped inside, the aroma of baking turkey and fruit pies enveloped him. In the next moment all he could think of was her.

She stood ramrod straight in the middle of the room, her back to him, her arms wrapped around herself. "Aw . . . hell, Jilly. I'm sorry."

She didn't turn. "Did you come here to make me cry?"

"No." He put his arms around her and eased her back against his chest. Her muscles quivered with exhaustion and the effort it took to keep her tears at bay.

He rested his cheek against her hair. "I knew you'd be missing her."

She released a shaky breath. "I do miss her. So much I . . ."

He tightened his grip, aching for her.

"I hate this, Jack. I hate that she's not here. It's not fair. It's not right."

"I know," he murmured, rubbing his cheek against her silky hair.

He turned her in his arms and gazed down at her tear-soaked eyes. He lifted his hands to her wet cheeks and caught the tears with his thumbs, brushing them gently away. "That's life, I guess. Sometimes it just plain sucks."

Her lips lifted, and he caressed the side of her face. "You're so beautiful."

She caught her breath. "Jack—"

"I know." Jack lowered his mouth and trailed it across her eyebrow, her cheekbone. "I shouldn't touch you . . . but then I look at you and . . . all my honorable intentions fly right out the window." He pressed his mouth to hers, deeply but softly. She sagged against him, curving her hands around his shoulder.

A moment later she pulled out of his arms, visibly trembling. "I need to check the pies. Excuse me."

Jill hurried to the kitchen, aware of Jack following behind her. She shouldn't have let him in. Not today, not when she was feeling so alone and vulnerable. How could she protect herself from him, if all she wanted to do was crawl into his arms and stay there forever?

With Jack there was no forever. She had to remember that.

Hands shaking, she crossed to the double ovens and checked the one with the pies, forcing herself to really look at them.

"It smells wonderful in here."

She swallowed past the lump in her throat. "Thanks. You know me and holidays."

"Yeah." He paused. "I do."

She cursed her choice of words, took the oven mitts from the drawer and slipped them on.

"Can I help?"

"I've got it. Thanks." She took the pies from the oven and set them on the counter to cool.

"You must be having company today."

"Yes." She sneaked a glance at him, then wished she hadn't. He stood just inside the doorway, big and handsome and male. And hungry. To belong, to not be alone.

He would deny both vehemently. But something in his eyes, something young and lost, told her she was right. An invitation for him to stay jumped to her tongue. Calling herself a fool, she swallowed it.

"Would you like a cup of coffee?" she asked instead.

"That'd be great." He walked to the sink, propped himself against the counter, and smiled at her. "Thanks."

Her pulse fluttered. His presence changed the atmosphere, she thought. Suddenly her kitchen, her house, felt filled. Suddenly it felt like a home. The way it did the minute Rebecca barreled through the front door.

And just as suddenly she felt like a woman. Alive and aware of her own body, her sexuality.

Get a grip, she told herself, getting a coffee mug from the cupboard. Her imagination was working on holiday overdrive. She'd been alone a long time, she missed Rebecca, she—

Ached for Jack.

Drawing her eyebrows together, she filled the mug, automatically adding a splash of milk and a sprinkle of sugar. She handed it to him, hoping he wouldn't notice how her fingers trembled. He took the mug, meeting her eyes. She told herself to look away, to break the contact with some light quip. Instead she gazed stupidly at him, their fingers touching around the warm mug.

"Just the way I like it," he murmured, taking the cup from her outstretched hand.

Color flew to her cheeks, and she drew away from him. But where could she go? He filled her senses, sending her heart and good reason spinning out of control. Dear Lord, what did she do now?

Turning away from him, she checked the turkey and basted it unnecessarily; the entire time she was aware of him watching her.

She couldn't soften toward him, she thought, sliding the bird back into the oven. She couldn't let down her guard. She couldn't be remembering how it had been between them when it had been good. If she did, she would be lost.

She slammed the oven door, swamped with memories. Memories of the two of them snuggling together, warm and sated from making love, of them laughing over a shared joke, of Jack holding her while she slept. Of the words they had flung at each other during that last, awful fight.

She drew a deep breath, slipped out of her oven mitts, and tossed them on the counter. Needing to do something with her hands, she poured herself a half cup of coffee, filled the rest of the mug with milk, and added two heaping teaspoons of sugar.

"Still like a little coffee with your sugar and milk, I see."

She met her eyes, then looked away. "I haven't outgrown it, but every so often I try."

Silence fell between them again. She checked the oven again, he sipped his coffee. From outside came the sound of children laughing. She winced at the sound and brought her coffee to her lips.

"Pretty day," she murmured, knowing the comment was inane, but wanting, needing to fill the awkward silence.

"Very." Jack rested against the counter. "Just like yesterday was. And the day before that."

"You sound like you wish it wasn't."

He met her eyes, then looked away, frowning. "I guess I do. I guess I long for a flat, gray sky and the threat of snow."

She set her mug on the counter. "Sounds like you're homesick for Iowa."

He tilted his face to the ceiling, then swung his gaze back to hers. "Sue called and urged me to come home."

"And now you wish you had."

"Yeah, I kind of do."

She was surprised by the admission. And by the things, the feelings, he left unsaid but couldn't completely hide.

"You didn't expect that, did you?" He made a sound of self-disgust. "The day she called, when I refused even to consider going home, Sue called me a selfish S.O.B. She said I was just like my father."

He swore and turned away from her to face the window. He brought his coffee cup to his lips, then set it back down without drinking. "I'm nothing like him. I vowed to myself I never would be."

Her heart turned over. She opened her mouth to say something comforting, to reassure him, then shut it as she realized she didn't know what to say or how to help him.

He shook his head. "Thanksgiving Day in Trotter Junction was usually cloudy. And cold, with the nip of winter in the air. By now they've had their first snow."

He spoke almost as if to himself, not looking away from the window. "I remember tromping through the cornfields, my boots crunching in the snow, the cold stinging my cheeks and hands." He smiled. "It felt good. I always liked the cold."

"Sounds like you miss it."

He met her eyes once more. "I do."

She touched his arm, stroking lightly. "So go home, Jack. Just get on a plane and go."

"It's not so simple."

"It is." She motioned to the wall phone. "Pick it up and dial the airline of your choice. Lord knows, I wish I could." She cleared her throat. "I wish I had your siblings, your nieces and nephews. I wish I had a family who spent holidays together. A family who wanted to be together."

He cupped her cheek in his palm. "I know, Jilly. But this thing between my father and me, it . . ." He shook his head. "You don't understand. You don't—"

"No, I don't." She covered his hand with her own. "But I'd like to. Talk to me, Jack. Tell me what happened."

He hesitated, and she curved her fingers more closely around his. "It's why you came here today, isn't it? Because you wanted to talk?"

"No." He searched her gaze. "I came here because I wanted to be with you." Her heart stopped, then started again with a vengeance. He moved his fingers against her cheek, stroking softly. "And because I couldn't stop thinking about you."

She drew in a ragged breath. "I need some air."

Without waiting for him to respond, she crossed to the sliding glass door that led out onto her small patio. She opened it and slipped outside, her heart beating so heavily, she thought she felt light-headed.

The breeze was mild; the sun bright. She tilted her face to its light, letting the warmth spill over her, letting the fresh breeze clear her head.

Jack followed her outside and came to stand beside her. She didn't look at him, she didn't trust herself to, and instead kept her eyes closed, her face lifted to the heavens.

"I got a card from my parents yesterday," she said. "A greeting card. Store-bought. It was signed, 'Love, Mother and Dad.' I didn't recognize the writing, and I suspect Mother or Dad's secretary sent it." She curled her fingers into tight fists. "They didn't send Rebecca a card. They're her grandparents, for Pete's sake.

She swung her gaze toward his. "Even as a child I had to make a place for myself. I had to make my own way. I hated my isolation. The alienation that I had no choice but to accept. Mom and Dad were busy, with their careers, their social lives, each other. They didn't have time to love me, even though that's what I wanted more than anything in the world. Every Christmas I used to ask Santa for the same thing. I never got it.

"And now"—her throat closed over the words, and she fought to clear it—"I'm alone again. I made a family, but I lost it."

Her eyes swam with tears, and she blinked against them, swamped with thoughts of Rebecca, of her failed marriage, and of how much she had loved and wanted Jack. "And here you are, you're creating your own isolation. You're alienating yourself from your family. From people who love you and want to be with you. Five years ago you alienated yourself from me. I don't understand."

He touched her cheek lightly, then dropped his hand. "From the time I was old enough to listen, my dad told me how I'd wrecked his life. How getting Mom pregnant was the biggest mistake he ever made, and how he had given up everything for me."

Jack frowned at the sky, as if back in Iowa and expecting to see slate instead of blue, then met her eyes once more. "Before he got married, my dad was the leader of a swing band. He was really good too. His band made a couple of recordings. He used to tell me stories about his days on the road, about playing for an audience." Jack fisted his fingers. "The first eighteen years of my life, those were the only times he smiled."

"Surely you're exaggerating. Surely he couldn't have been—"

"So sour? So bitter?" He met her eyes, his bright with anger. But not anger directed at her, she realized. At his father, for all he'd done, but more, for those things he hadn't done. "Christmas mornings my dad didn't get up with us. He didn't get up until all the presents had been opened and all the debris had been cleared away."

Jill sank onto one of the wrought-iron patio chairs, her heart pounding, her mouth dry. Jack didn't sit; he prowled. She folded her hands in her lap and watched him, letting him take his time, understanding how difficult this was for him.

"Eighteen birthdays I celebrated in that house. My dad wasn't home for one of them. Not one." Jack's mouth twisted. "Whenever one of us had a birthday, he stayed out all night. To punish Mom for having us. To punish us for having been born, for ruining his life."

Her stomach turned over. "What about your mother?" she asked softly. "Why did she—"

"Stay with him?" She nodded. "Out of guilt, I think. After all, as he was fond of saying, he gave up everything for her." His expression softened. "She did the best she could. She tried to make the various holidays festive and full of joy. Same with our birthdays. She loved us all a lot. But some things can't be made up for. Whenever he wasn't there, we felt his absence keenly, even more than we would have felt his presence."

She swallowed hard, hurting for him, wishing there was something she could say to ease his pain but knowing there wasn't.

Jack shook his head, eyes squinting against the light.

"He hated his life. And yet he wanted the same thing for me. He gave up on his dreams, and he expected me to give up on mine."

She sat forward in her chair. "What do you mean?"

Anger crossed his features. "I wanted to come out here. Go to film school at Berkeley. I'd worked damn hard, my grades were top-notch. I got accepted." He met her eyes, the expression in his chilled her. "He laughed. He called me a fool. He told me I'd never amount to anything."

"Oh, Jack."

"My whole life, everything I did or wanted was wrong. I was never good enough." Jack flexed his fingers. "You know what he wanted me to do? Graduate from high school and go to work in the factory with him."

Jill stood and walked to him, aching for the proud and hurt young man Jack had been. And for the one he was now. "So you left."

"I told him I was going. I told him that my dreams would come true because I believed in myself. Because I would make them happen." Jack shook his head. "He said he'd talk to me when I came crawling back on my belly. He said maybe he'd let me come back home . . . if I begged. I decided then and there that hell would freeze over before I went back."

She cupped his face in her palms. "He sounds like an unhappy person. I feel—"

"Don't feel sorry for him. He doesn't deserve your pity."

She moved her fingers over Jack's face, bleeding for him. So proud, so stubborn. So much time lost that would never be regained. "I don't feel sorry for him. I feel sorry for the little boy who must have loved him very much."

For a moment Jack said nothing. "If I ever loved him, it was so long ago that I've forgotten."

Jill gazed at him, emotion choking her. He'd opened up to her, she realized. For the first time he'd shared his innermost feelings, a bit of his heart. For the first time she understood part of what made Jack the man he was.

She loved him.

The realization rocketed through her, stealing her breath away, her ability to think. Dear God, she loved him. Still. Even with everything she'd known about him from the past, even with everything she'd learned today. She loved him.

Fear bloomed inside her, icy cold and debilitating. She swung away from him. He believed in her, in her abilities. He had confidence in her; he trusted and liked her. But he had never loved her. What was she going to do? How was she going to keep him from hurting her?

She searched for something to say, for something that would change her feelings. Nothing would, she knew. Five years and a world of regrets hadn't changed them, how could mere words?

Peter had been right. She'd never stopped loving Jack.

She brought a hand to her throat, then dropped it. "I need to . . . check the turkey. Excuse me."

She turned and ran inside. She reached the kitchen and the oven and stared blankly at it. *She loved him.* She pressed her hands to her burning cheeks. What was she doing? What was she thinking? She couldn't love him.

He would never love her back.

She made a sound of pain. She couldn't change the way she felt. It was too late. Too late—

"Jilly?" She heard Jack step inside, heard him slide the door shut behind him. "Are you all right?"

She didn't turn. Didn't respond. She couldn't. She squeezed her eyes shut. Dear Lord, what did she do now?

He crossed the room, stopping directly behind her. He touched her hair lightly. "Did I say something that upset you? Did I do something that . . . hurt you?"

He had hurt her—terribly. *In the past.*

But in the past he'd never opened up to her. He'd never shared himself, his feelings. Today he had.

The truth of that hit her in a dizzying wave. If he shared himself with her, there was hope. A chance he would love her, a chance for them together. Slim, but a chance nonetheless. Joy exploded inside her, crowding out her fear, pushing at her uncertainties.

"Jilly?"

He touched her hair again, and she bit her lip. "You didn't say or do anything wrong, Jack. It's me."

"I don't understand."

She turned. Trembling, she placed her hands on his chest. Heat emanated from him. Under the light weave of his sweater, his heart thundered.

She gazed up at him, her own heart beating so wildly, she thought she might faint. "I want us to make love. I want us to be lovers."

"Jilly—" He sucked in a quick, sharp breath. "Do you know what you're saying? What you're doing?"

Did she? She searched her heart, her soul. The damage had already been done; protecting herself from loving him was an impossibility. He owned her heart already.

And nothing had felt so right, so perfect, in a long time.

"Yes," she whispered, standing on tiptoe, pressing herself against him. "I want us to be lovers. Do you want the same thing?"

"How can you even ask?" He cupped her face in his hard palms. "I want you so much, I can hardly breathe. I go to sleep thinking of you, of being with you. I awaken the same way."

She tilted her face up to his. "Then don't make me wait any longer."

He didn't. With an urgency born of need he caught her mouth. Their tongues met and mated. He wound his fingers in her hair, dragging her closer.

She wondered what an hour from now would bring, how a week from now would find her. She shoved the thoughts roughly aside. She had waited such a long time to be with him again. So long, it seemed like forever. She wouldn't spoil it with worries—tomorrow would take care of itself.

He swept her into his arms. "Where?" he muttered against her mouth.

"Upstairs, my bedroom. That way."

He took the stairs quickly, more quickly than she could have thought possible while carrying her. Her bedroom was dark, the drapes still closed against the light. Jack crossed to the windows and yanked open the drapes. Sunlight spilled through, warm and brilliant white, soaking the room, the bed. Soaking them.

He carried her to the unmade bed and together they fell onto the rumpled bedding. Jack caught her mouth and with a boldness that took her breath, parted her lips. She met his kiss just as boldly, tangling her tongue with his. They made low, hungry sounds, sounds of urgency, of need too long denied.

Anxious for the feel of his skin against her hands, she struggled with his clothing, pushing at it, as he did hers. They separated long enough for her to work his sweater over his head, then came back together, clutching at each other as if they'd been forced apart for ages instead of seconds.

Jack followed her lead, yanking her T-shirt over her head. Beneath his hands her skin was smooth and as warm as fresh cream. He traced his fingers almost reverently across her collarbone, over her shoulders and upper arms.

He brought his mouth to the places he'd just explored with his fingers, delighting in the way she arched and moaned. He'd waited so long. To touch and taste her. To hear his name on her lips in the throes of passion. He'd missed her, more than he'd even realized until this moment. No woman had ever moved him the way Jill did. No woman had ever touched him.

The thought brought a ripple of unease, a warning. He ignored it and instead eased her to her back. Resting on his elbows, he gazed down at her. "You're so beautiful," he murmured. She flushed, and his lips curved up. "I especially like that shade of pink."

With his fingertips only, he traced long, lazy shapes across her rosy skin, across the lacy brassiere that partially hid her breasts from him. As he did, her nipples peaked and pressed against the lace.

He slipped a finger beneath the fabric, teasing the nubbin, then drew his hand away. Jill clutched the bedding, aching for more, for his mouth and tongue. He continued to torment her instead, simply admiring, stroking, cupping, brushing his mouth ever so softly against her flesh.

Finally, with a sound of need she wound her fingers in his hair and brought his face fully to her breasts. He didn't disappoint her. He unfastened the front clasp of her bra, and a moment later brought his mouth and hands fully to her.

Shudders rippled over her, and she arched, straining against him. "Jack . . . Jack . . . I need you." She worked at the snap of his jeans, unfastening it. Her fingers found the zipper and pulled it down. He returned the favor, fumbling at the button of her shorts, working them over her hips.

Naked, finally, they fell against each other, warm flesh to warm flesh. The sensation was incredible, and Jill moved her hands over him. Exploring. Relearning. Once, she had known his body almost as well as her own. The way his skin felt under her fingers, the way it warmed to her touch. She'd known his planes and angles, had known which muscles flexed and bunched during lovemaking, had known what he liked best.

As she explored, her sensory memory came alive, more alive with each second that passed, alive for the first time in five years. He hadn't changed much. His body was harder, fuller. A man's body now, fully mature, powerful.

She moved her mouth with her hands, tasting, absorbing his texture with her lips and tongue, giving and receiving pleasure.

She stopped on a deep indention in his side. She ran her index finger over it lightly. "What's this?" she asked, her voice husky, tipping her face up to his.

"A scar. It's nothing."

"It's not nothing. This is a big mark." She drew her eyebrows together. "How did you get it?"

"Two years ago," he murmured, holding her face in his palm, "I was downtown . . . a guy tried to mug me. He had a knife and—"

"A knife!" she repeated, beginning to tremble. "You could have been killed."

He drew her up to him and cradled her body against his. "But I wasn't killed. It was a glancing blow. A flesh wound, that's all."

A flesh wound, she thought, shuddering. Jack's flesh. She could have lost him. And she would have had to read it in the papers. Or heard it through the grapevine.

Tears stung her eyes, and she battled them. "Where were you when it happened? Was it night? Or day? Was anyone with—"

"It doesn't matter." He brushed his mouth against hers. "I'm fine, Jilly, sweet. I'm fine."

"It does matter," she said fiercely. "Someone hurt you."

"Thank you for caring," he whispered, kissing her.

She curved her arms around him. "I don't want to wait any longer, Jack. Make love to me."

"But you haven't—"

"No." She laid her fingers against his lips. "I don't want anything but you inside me."

He searched her expression, his own strained with control. "You're sure this is what you want?"

She moved against him. "Can't you tell? It's what I want. The only thing I want."

His restraint snapped. She saw it in his eyes, felt it in the way his body quivered. "Wait," he said hoarsely. "One minute."

He reached over the side of the bed, fumbling for his jeans and wallet. After he'd found what he searched for and slipped it on, he returned to her.

Jill gazed at him, several different emotions warring inside her. Not the least of which was hurt. Because of their past, because of the words they had flung at each other all those years ago. "I wouldn't try to trap you," she whispered.

"I know." He drew her into his arms and kissed her, slowly and deeply. "But I don't take any chances, my sweet. Not ever."

"So you carry something around with you, just in case."

He smiled against her mouth, at her tone. "I like it when you're jealous, and yes I carry one everywhere. But be reassured, love. It's been in my wallet for a very long time."

She lifted her lips. "Months and months?"

He laughed softly and rolled her onto her back. "More than that. Much more." He poised over her, his smile fading. "You're so beautiful, Jilly. So special. I've missed you."

She wrapped her legs around his, her heart thrumming, joy and desire mingling inside her, creating an intoxicating mixture. There was hope for them. This time she and Jack had a real chance at a happy ending.

I love you.

The words sprang to her lips. She swallowed them, even though it hurt to do so. She longed to tell him everything she felt. But if she did, she knew, he would be out of her house so fast, it would make her head spin.

"I need you," she said instead, moving against him.

Slowly, his eyes never leaving hers, he entered her.

Pleasure rocketed through her. She gasped and tightened her arms and legs, holding onto him, vowing to never let him go.

They moved together, slowly at first, their tension and passion building, spiraling past control, beyond reason. Jill cried out Jack's name; he caught it with his mouth, making his own sounds of pleasure, of release.

Jack collapsed against her, murmuring her name, raining kisses over her face. They lay that way for a long time, holding each other, each lost in their own thoughts, their own hopes and fears. Their flesh cooled and hearts slowed. Jack eased them onto their sides. He gazed at her, his chest full with emotion. Tenderness nearly overwhelmed him, and he pushed the dampened tendrils of hair away from her flushed face.

How had he ever let her go?

And how, now that he'd held her again, would he face a future without her?

He'd promised himself he wouldn't become involved with her again. He'd vowed that he wouldn't allow her to turn him inside out and backward again. And here he was, so tipped and turned that he didn't know which way was up. Or what was right.

"You're just like Dad, you know that Jack?"

He wasn't, Jack thought, tension stiffening at the back of his neck. And he never would be.

She opened her eyes and looked at him. Alarm—and hurt—raced into her face. "Don't," she whispered. "No regrets. Not already."

"I didn't come here for this."

"I know." Her lips curved and she smoothed her hands over his shoulders. "If you had, you'd be out on your ear."

He tangled his fingers in her hair, spread out across the pillow. "You're incredible."

Pleasure colored her cheeks. "Thanks. So are you."

He rubbed some strands of her hair between his fingers. They felt like silk against his skin. "What time is your company coming?"

"Four."

"Can I stay?"

"Of course." She drew her eyebrows together. "Did you really think I'd boot you out?"

"I thought maybe . . . that maybe you had someone coming who—" He cleared his throat, annoyed at how difficult he found this. Unnerved by how much he hated the idea of her with another man. "That it might be awkward for me to be here."

"Because I had a date?"

"Yes."

She smiled. "I have friends coming today. Just friends. About a dozen of them actually."

He smiled, relief and self-satisfaction curling through him. "There's no other man in your life? No one special?"

"And if I said there was?" she teased.

He mock-growled. "I'd be forced to do something drastic."

"Drastic? Hmm . . ." She laced her fingers around the back of his neck and arched ever so slightly, just so the tips of her breasts rubbed against his chest. "Sounds interesting."

He tumbled her to her back. "You think so, do you? You're a cruel woman, Jill Lansing."

She smiled up at him and batted her eyelashes in exaggerated innocence. "Who me?"

"Mmm-hmm." He laughed and sat up, pinning her with his arms and legs. "And you're also good at avoiding answering questions." He leaned toward her. "So, is there someone else in the picture?"

"And if I refuse to answer?"

"I tickle you to death. It's a simple choice."

Her smile faded. She reached up and stroked his cheek. "There's no one else, Jack. If there were, I wouldn't be here."

Relief swelled inside him. Along with something else, something warm and sweet. Something that made him want never to let her go. He bent and pressed his mouth to hers.

They made love again, this time slowly, with infinite tenderness. Both took the time to please and be pleased, touching, stroking, murmuring words of appreciation, of affection.

They weren't the words Jill wanted to murmur, they weren't the ones she wanted to hear. But she contented herself with the certainty that Jack cared for her. That there was a chance for them.

The light changed, mellowed; shadows eased into the corners of the room, the edges of the bed. Jill glanced at the clock and made a sound of despair.

"What's wrong?" Jack asked sleepily.

"It's almost three." She threw the covers aside and scrambled out of bed. "I'll never have everything done in time."

"What do you have left to do?"

"Don't ask, there's so much." She groaned and pushed the hair out of her eyes, searching for her clothes. "This is a disaster."

"I'll help." He climbed out of bed and reached for his jeans. "Just tell me what to do."

"Right." She pulled on her shorts and scrambled to find her T-shirt. "I've seen you in the kitchen."

"That was five years ago." He slipped his sweater over his head and grinned. "I think I'm going to surprise you."

EIGHT

Jack did surprise her. He ran the vacuum while she cleaned the potatoes, stuffed the celery while she arranged the canapés on a tray, set up the bar while she put the finishing touches on the buffet table.

She smiled to herself and shook her head as he slipped on her frilly apron and dug into the sink full of dirty pots and pans. Five years ago he wouldn't have been caught dead stuffing celery let alone wearing an apron. His machismo couldn't have taken it. Today he not only approached the domestic tasks competently and good-naturedly, but he actually seemed to be enjoying himself.

Did Jack realize how much he'd changed in the past five years? she wondered, tilting her head, studying him. Did he realize how those changes heightened his appeal?

He looked up and caught her staring at him. He grinned. "What? Never seen a man up to his elbows in dishwater before?"

She returned his smile. "Just not this man."

He took his hands out of the sudsy water and blew

her a kiss, spraying bubbles across the room. "If you wait long enough, anything can happen."

Could it? she wondered twenty minutes later as she sat in front of her dressing-table mirror, putting the final touches on her cursory makeup job. If she waited long enough, would he love her? Would he realize he wanted to spend his life with her, that he wanted to be a father and a grandfather?

"You look beautiful."

She lifted her gaze. Jack stood in the doorway of her dressing room, his eyes on her, dark with awareness.

Heat crept up her cheeks. "Thanks. So do you."

He crossed the room and stopped behind her, putting his hands on her shoulders. He'd showered, too, and smelled of her brand of soap and shampoo. It mingled with his own unique, male scent, and she breathed deeply, excited by the intimacy of the situation and by knowing that for this moment he was hers.

Jack leaned toward her, his eyes still on hers in the mirror. He moved his fingers in slow, rhythmic sweeps across her shoulders. "You can't imagine how much restraint it took to keep from climbing into the shower with you."

She drew in a strangled breath. Her nipples peaked, pressing almost painfully against her silk blouse. She could imagine them there, the warm water sluicing over their naked bodies. "Can't I?" she whispered. "Don't be so sure."

He slid his hands over her shoulders and dipped them into the deep vee of her blouse, cupping her bare breasts. "I ache for you."

The heat in her cheeks became fire. She shuddered and leaned her head back against him, his arousal. He moved his hands against her flesh, stroking, caressing, igniting flames at the center of her.

She covered his hands and tipped her head back; he bent his and caught her parted lips. The doorbell rang. Disappointment, so sharp it stung, speared through her. She groaned, low in her throat.

He smiled against her mouth. "Let them wait."

The urge to do just that rushed over her, shocking her. She pictured her and Jack making love, here on her dressing-room floor, the doorbell ringing, over and over. Pictured her friends at the front gate wondering where she was and if something had happened to her.

"I can't," she whispered even as she tightened her hands over his, unwilling to let him go.

"I know." He kissed her again passionately, then drew away from her. "We'd better answer that."

She shivered and hugged herself, cold without his hands. "Or they'll know what we've been up to."

He eased her to her feet. "There'll be no question what we've been up to, no matter what we do. You look like a woman who was caught in the middle of making love."

She brought her hands to her flushed cheeks, embarrassed, knowing he was right but uncertain what to do about it.

He laughed softly and laced their fingers together. Tugging on her hand, he galvanized her into motion. "Come on. I'm only teasing, no one will know. Unless of course we keep them waiting any longer."

Dana knew. She arrived with her date—a handsome young man Jill had never met before—shortly after the first group of guests, and Jill saw the surprise, then the speculation, in her eyes as she observed her and Jack.

Jill dodged both for as long as she could. Finally Dana caught and cornered her in the kitchen.

"You and Jack have decided to get along, I see." Dana leaned against the counter, all but giggling. "What a surprise."

Cheeks burning, Jill glared at the other woman. "Can it, Dana."

Her friend laughed. "Testy, aren't we?"

"Busy," Jill corrected, sliding a tray of canapés out of the oven. "So, why don't you run along and play. I'll be out in a moment."

Dana ignored her and selected a canapé. She blew on it to cool it, then took a bite, murmuring her appreciation. "You're the best cook."

Jill removed her oven mitts and tossed them on the counter. "Thanks."

"When did it happen?"

"It?"

"Yes, you know. *It.* With a capital *I.* You and Jack."

Jill made a sound of frustration. She couldn't hide a thing from Dana, dammit. She glanced over her shoulder to make sure none of the other guests was within earshot. "Today. Okay? But don't worry, it won't affect our work."

"Do I look worried?" Dana smiled, and selected another hors d'oeuvre. "Actually I think this is the way it's supposed to be. Any two people who have as much chemistry between them as you and Jack do belong together."

"Thanks for the vote of confidence. Unfortunately, though, the future isn't in your and my hands only. And I have Rebecca to think of."

"Jack seems like the kind of guy who would be good with kids."

Jill thought of the afternoon at the Playland, of the little bear he had brought Rebecca, and of the way her daughter had taken to him so quickly. A smile touched her mouth. "Rebecca really likes him. And she did right off, which isn't like her. She's usually slower to warm up."

"See." Dana reached for another canapé, then, as if reconsidering, dropped her hand. "Perfect daddy material."

Jill's smile faded. "You may think so, but Jack has other ideas."

"What does that mean?"

"It means Jack never intends—" Jill shook her head. "Forget it. I don't want to talk about my love life right now. I'd rather talk about yours."

Dana shifted her gaze to the tray of hors d'oeuvres. "Mine? What do you mean?"

"Don't be coy." Jill began transferring the canapés from the baking sheet to the tray. "Tell me about this hunk you brought with you today. Someone new?"

"Kind of." She tried to laugh and failed miserably.

"Kind of?" Jill repeated, arching her eyebrows at her friend's evasion. "You never mentioned him before."

"I know." Dana sighed. "Paul and I met three months ago. We're crazy about each other."

Jill shook her head. "No wonder you look and sound so miserable."

Dana crumpled her cocktail napkin. "I didn't say anything because"—she took a deep breath—"I'm afraid the entire station's going to laugh at me."

"Laugh at you? Why? Because you have a knock-down gorgeous guy? Please."

"Now you're the one who's being coy. Isn't it obvious why I might feel . . . ridiculous about a relationship between me and Paul?"

"No. Why?"

"I'm too old for him."

"Oh, Dana, you're not—"

"Yes, I am." She began shredding the crumpled napkin. "Nine years, Jill. There's nine years between us. Almost ten. Not to mention the difference in the places we are in our lives and careers."

Jill saw the way her friend battled tears. Her heart went out to her. She touched Dana's arm lightly. "Does it bother you that much?"

Dana shook her head and drew in a shaky breath. "Not enough to stop seeing him. He makes me happy. He makes me laugh." She glanced down at her hands, then back up at Jill. "It isn't just a physical thing. There's something between us, something that fills my heart with . . ."

Her words trailed off, and Jill covered her hand. "Then forget about the rest, Dana. If he makes you feel good, don't let him get away. Fight for him."

"Easy for you to say, Jill." Dana pushed away from the counter, her tears brimming, her cheeks bright. "Apply that same advice to your own love affair and see how it feels. Excuse me."

For the rest of the evening Jill couldn't shake Dana's last words to her or the way they had made her feel. Like a fraud. Like there was something right in front of her but she couldn't see it.

Was it easy for her? she wondered as she circled the

room, chatting with friends. Was she glibly giving Dana advice when she couldn't look with any clarity at her own life? Being with Jack made her happy. And unhappy. Just the way being with Paul made Dana feel.

She looked past the woman she was talking to, searching for Jack. She found him sitting on the couch, having a conversation with her editor from the *Times*. Her heart turned over. Had she been wrong leaving him all those years ago? She'd loved him; he'd made her happy. Yet she'd walked out because she'd wanted everything; she'd wanted a perfect relationship, a perfect life. She hadn't been willing to fight for him.

Was she willing to fight now?

Jack looked up at her then. He didn't smile, didn't acknowledge her in any way, yet she curled her fingers around the back of the chair at the expression in his eyes. Hot and possessive, his gaze seemed to say: *"I want you. I wish we were alone. You're mine."*

Her knees went weak. Yes, she would fight for him. This time she wouldn't run; she wouldn't give up. This time he would love her.

The remainder of the evening passed in a blur. Her thoughts stayed with her, as did the memory of the look in Jack's eyes. The food was delicious, the company enjoyable; she wanted everyone out of her house so that she could be alone with Jack.

She couldn't keep her eyes off him. As the minutes passed, the knot of desire inside her tightened. She had no idea what she talked about with her friends, no idea even which friends she'd spoken to.

Murmuring what seemed like the millionth "excuse me" of the night, Jill lifted her gaze, finding Jack looking at her. He smiled, the curving of his lips male, predatory, full of sensual promise. She returned his smile, making delicious promises of her own.

He murmured something to the person he was conversing with, and started toward her. She watched him, her mouth dry, her heart fast. He moved easily and confidently through the room, drawing the attention of every female within shouting distance, a man sure of himself and of his own power.

His power over her.

He stopped beside her. "When are these people going to leave?" he whispered next to her ear. "Don't they have homes?"

"Would it be rude to ask?" She smiled. "Or we could pretend to be out of liquor."

"They'd only ask for more coffee and pie."

She laughed. "Cynic."

"I've got an idea."

"So do I. But it might get us arrested."

"Not that kind of idea, vixen." He bent and brushed his mouth against hers. "I'm going to enlist a little help. Be right back."

Moments later he returned with Dana and her date in tow. Laughter in her eyes, Dana held out her hand. "I had a wonderful time, Jill. Thank you so much for inviting us."

Jill shifted her gaze to Jack's and took Dana's hand, a bit confused. "You have to go?"

"Oh, yes," she said a bit louder. "It is getting late, and I know you have things to do . . . tomorrow."

Jill understood then and smiled. "I'm glad you two could make it." She walked her friends to the door. "Thanks for coming, Dana." She turned to Paul and smiled. "It was great to meet you, Paul. Have Dana bring you by again."

He thanked her and Jack, then before they left, Jill kissed Dana's cheek. "Thanks for the words of advice," she whispered. "You were right."

Dana frowned, confused. "But I didn't give you—"

"Yes, you did. In a roundabout way." She smiled at her friend's obvious confusion. "I'll tell you about it another time."

"Whatever you say." Dana shrugged into her lightweight coat. "Thanks again. I'll see you at the station next week."

Jack's plan worked. No sooner had Dana left than her other guests began following suit. Within thirty minutes she and Jack were alone.

They fell into each other's arms. "You're a genius," she murmured, pressing kisses over his face and neck. "I thought we would never be alone."

"Not a genius . . . just a man on a desperate mission." He buried his face in her hair. "God, I thought I was going to die from wanting you."

"Me too." She tilted her head back, and he plundered her neck with his lips and tongue. "It was agony."

"No more waiting—"

"Thank God."

They tugged at each other's clothing, struggling with buttons and zippers and clinging fabric. A button went sailing, a seam rent; her silk blouse floated to the floor.

Finally, after what seemed like eons apart, they came together, warm flesh to warm flesh. They sank to the carpet.

"Don't go slow," she murmured against his mouth,

moving her hands over his bare chest. "Don't make me wait."

"I won't, love." He rolled onto his back, bringing her with him. "I couldn't."

She rained kisses over his shoulders and chest. She felt his urgency in the slick heat of his skin and the thunder of his heart, in the way his arousal strained against her.

Grasping her hips, he guided her onto him. She was ready, warm and aching. She arched her back, a low sound of pleasure slipping past her parted lips.

They made love with a fury born of need, with the frenetic passion that was such an inexplicable part of their reaction to each other.

When it was over, Jill collapsed against his chest, breathless and sated. Jack curved his arms around her, cradling her against him.

"Tired?" he asked softly, pressing a kiss to her hair.

"Mmm." She snuggled into his arms. "Exhausted."

"Do you want me to stay the night?"

She lifted her head and met his eyes, surprised by his question. Five years ago he would have assumed she wanted him to stay. But then, five years ago they hadn't had so much past between them.

"Yes," she whispered. "I want you to stay. But only if you really want to."

His lips curved up, and he eased onto his side, bringing her with him so that they nestled face-to-face. "I do."

She returned his smile. "I'm glad. And Jack?"

"Hmm?"

"You don't have to ask again."

❧————————————————❧

Light burned the back of his eyes. Jack groaned sleepily and shifted, his limbs feeling heavy and leaden.

"Wake up, sleepyhead."

Jack cracked open his eyes. Jill sat on the edge of the bed, fully awake and dressed, a mug of steaming coffee in her hand. He groaned again. "Who opened the blinds?"

"Yours truly. Of course."

Laughter tinged her voice and he tugged the pillow over his face. "You're a heartless and vicious woman."

"We all have to be good at something."

He lifted the pillow to glare at her. "What time is it?"

"Nearly eight." She smiled and took a sip of her coffee. "Time to get up."

He groaned again and moved his gaze over her. "You're dressed."

"Yup. And showered." She took another sip of her coffee. "Disappointed?"

"What do you think?" He pulled himself into a sitting position and reached for her coffee, taking the cup from her. "How can I ravish your body with you all bundled up like that?"

"Good point. But I didn't want us to be late."

"Late?" He brought the mug to his lips, sipped, and made a face at its sweetness. "Late for what?"

She leaned toward him. "The mall of course. Today's the official start of the holiday shopping season."

"Great. Wake up only to be sentenced to hell." He took another healthy sip of her coffee, feeling the kick of the caffeine. He eyed her warily. "What other forms of torture have you included on your Thanksgiving week-end schedule?"

"Well . . . since Rebecca's gone until Sunday evening, I thought this would be the perfect time—"

"To stay in bed and make love all day." He grinned and reached for her. "Excellent plan."

She slapped his hands playfully away. "No. I thought this would be the perfect time to hit Toys "R" Us. After all, Rebecca's been a very good girl this year."

"And you intend to spoil her rotten."

"Of course. You've got a problem with that?"

"Who me?" He arched his eyebrows in exaggerated disbelief. "No way."

She reached for the coffee, forehead wrinkled in thought. "How good are you at putting together kids' toys?"

"That depends."

"She wants one of those motorized Jeeps. You know, one of the ones you can ride in. The pink, Barbie model."

"The 'pink, Barbie model'?" he repeated, laughing. He lifted his hands in mock terror. "That sounds tough."

"Smart aleck."

"Who me?" He said with exaggerated innocence, and relieved her of the coffee cup. "What else is on your holiday-from-hell schedule?"

"A couple of new Christmas features open today, and I'm reviewing them for my next column."

"Okay." He drained the last of the coffee and set the cup on the nightstand. "What about getting a tree and decorating the house? You always do that this weekend. It's a tradition."

Her smile slipped. "Now I have a new tradition. I do those things with Rebecca."

She started to stand, but he caught her hand, stopping her. His eyes were soft with regret. "Hell, Jilly . . . I'm sorry. I forgot."

She gazed at him a moment, then sighed and shifted her gaze. "So did I. Yesterday and last night. For a few minutes this morning.

"Hey." Jack laced their fingers together. "Is that a crime?"

"I'm her mother."

"Does that mean you can't be just a woman for a few hours?" He smiled softly and eased her down beside him. "That's a little unnatural, don't you think?"

"You don't understand. You're not her father . . . you don't love her. You're not afraid you're going to lose her."

Jack stiffened. "No, I'm not her father," he said evenly. "But I don't have to be to know that thinking about your daughter every minute is not what makes you a good mother. And I also know that worrying over the custody battle every waking moment is not going to influence the judge's decision."

Jill rested her face against his chest, acknowledging that he was right, that she was being overly sensitive, reactionary. Because she was scared. She released her pent-up breath on a sigh. "How'd you get to be so smart?"

He threaded his fingers through her hair. "Like you said, I have a little distance from this situation."

She tipped her face up to his. "I'm sorry."

"You have nothing to be sorry about, Jilly."

"Yeah, I do. What I said to you . . . it wasn't fair."

He brought his mouth to hers, kissing her gently but deeply. "That's okay," he murmured, drawing a fraction of an inch away. "I can take it."

She smiled and tangled her fingers in his hair. "Then do."

With a sound of pleasure he did just that.

The rest of the weekend passed in a whirl. Jack, with a minimum of cursing and smashed thumbs, put together Rebecca's Jeep and the huge dollhouse he had insisted Rebecca couldn't live without. They'd eaten leftovers, fought the crush at the mall, and gone to the Christmas features Jill needed to review. One of the movies was nothing short of remarkable, and they did the impossible—agreed that a new holiday classic had been born.

The most memorable part of the weekend, however, was their lovemaking. They'd made love so many times and with such sweet abandon that Jill had lost count.

By Sunday afternoon they were both exhausted. Jill checked her watch, smiled, and leaned against the sofa. Rebecca would be home in a little less than two hours. That gave her and Jack time to eat, then make leisurely love before they said good-bye.

She closed her eyes and smiled. Other than missing Rebecca, the weekend had been perfection. She and Jack had talked and laughed and simply enjoyed being with each other. It had reminded her of the way it had been between them way back at the beginning of their relationship.

She heard the front door close, heard the sound of Jack bounding up the stairs. She turned and smiled at him as he came into the room carrying a pizza box. "The answer to the too-many-leftovers blues."

She grinned. "My hero."

He crossed to her and set the pizza on the old blanket she'd spread over the carpet, and opened the box with a flourish. "As you instructed, with everything but anchovies."

They dug into the pie, but before Jack took his first bite, he stopped and looked at her in astonishment. "You're drinking beer."

She arched an eyebrow. "Women do."

"But you hate the stuff."

"I used to. I'm developing a taste for it. I love it with pizza."

He reached across the blanket and laid a hand on her forehead. "No fever. But what if it's catching anyway?" He shuddered in mock horror. "I'll find myself liking overbaked, sappy movies. It would be a disaster."

She crumpled her napkin and tossed it at him. "You've got a problem with becoming a better reviewer? Strange man."

He laughed and tumbled her against him. "Be nice, or I won't share my pizza."

"Your pizza!"

"I paid for it."

"My house."

"Witch."

"Tyrant."

He caught her laughter with his mouth. He kissed her long and hard, then released her. "All this banter is making me hungry." He reached for a slice and took a big bite.

She laughed again and shook her head. "You must be

getting old. There was a time our bantering made you feel . . . romantic."

"Not old," he corrected. "Aged. Like a fine wine."

She reached for a slice of the pizza. "Oh, please. Like a fine wine?"

He arched his eyebrows. "What else?"

"A moldy, old cheese."

He growled. "You'll pay for that, Jill Lansing."

"After you're done eating," she teased.

"Right. We old people have our priorities."

The rest of their meal passed in companionable silence, each lost in their own thoughts. When they'd both eaten more than they should have, Jill made a sound of satisfaction and leaned back against the couch. "I couldn't eat another bite if my life depended on it."

"Great pizza." Jack tossed the rest of a slice back into the box. "But I'm with you. No more." He tumbled her against his chest, smiling wickedly. "When is Rebecca due back?"

She arched into him, practically purring her contentment. "In a little over an hour. That should give us enough time."

He tangled his fingers in her hair and lowered his mouth until it hovered just above hers. "For what, my wicked little vixen?"

He knew exactly "what for," but she played along, enjoying their sexy banter. "To make love," she murmured, catching his mouth, then retreating. "One more time before you leave."

Jack's mouth stilled on hers, and he drew a little bit away. "Before I leave?" he repeated.

"Mmm . . ." She brushed her mouth across his. "Before Peter gets here with Rebecca."

"Oh." Jack stiffened. "I didn't understand that I was leaving so soon."

She straightened, then eased out of his arms, feeling cold without him. She rubbed her arms against the chill. "But you knew Rebecca would be back this afternoon. You knew that Peter was bringing her home."

He drew his eyebrows together, his expression tense. "Oh, yeah, I knew that. What I didn't know was that you wanted me out of here before she got home."

"It's not Rebecca," she said, surprised. "It's Peter."

"Peter."

"Yes."

Now he looked furious. She swore silently. She'd taken for granted that, considering her ex-husband's feelings about him and her worries over the impending custody hearing, Jack would understand her not wanting him and Peter to come face-to-face. Obviously he didn't.

She stood and nervously began collecting the remnants of their meal, aware of Jack's eyes upon her. Not yet prepared for the argument she knew she couldn't avoid, she headed toward the kitchen, her hands full. Crossing to the sink, she put the plates and glasses in it, then turned on the water.

He followed her to the kitchen and set the pizza box on the counter. He leaned against it, facing her. "You want me to go because you don't want Peter to see me."

She ran a plate under the stream of warm water. "If you don't mind, yes."

"But I do mind. I mind a hell of a lot." He reached around her and flipped off the water. Her heart sank, but she turned and met his gaze evenly. "Are you embarrassed by me?"

"No!" She shook her head, astounded that he could think such a thing. "Of course not."

He slipped his hands into the front pockets of his blue jeans. "Are we doing something wrong here?"

She caught her bottom lip between her teeth. "No . . ."

Frowning, he searched her gaze. "You don't sound, or look, convinced. You were always a terrible liar, Jilly."

"It's not that." She shook her head. "I don't think we're doing anything wrong. But I'm afraid Peter would disagree."

"You're not allowed to date?" Jack arched his eyebrows in disbelief. "He's allowed to remarry, but you can't date?"

She squeezed her fingers into fists. "Of course I can date. It's just that I wouldn't want him to think, you know, that we . . ."

"That we're lovers."

"Yes."

"But we are."

Her cheeks colored. "I have Rebecca to think about. With this custody battle hanging over my head, I can't give Peter anything he might use against me. And when it comes to you, he's completely—"

Her buzzer rang. She looked at the clock, frowned, then answered the call. Her heart sank when she heard her ex-husband's voice. She told him she would be down in a moment, hung up, and turned to Jack. "Peter's here. He's early." She caught her bottom lip between her teeth. "He's never early."

"It's fate, then."

She looked at Jack, begging for understanding with

her eyes. "Please, Jack. I don't want him to know you're here."

"What do you want me to do? Sneak out the back way like a criminal or hide in the bedroom like a wimp?"

"It's not like that."

"Bull."

"He never comes up. Just don't let him know you're here." She twisted her fingers together. "Please. For me."

He made a sound of frustration—and capitulation. "This sucks, Jill. We're not doing anything wrong."

"It's you, Jack. He hates you. I told you what he thought when we were married, and if he knows that you and I, that now we're . . ."

She let the words trail off, and Jack swore. "Okay, Jill. This time. But don't expect me to hide every time your ex comes around."

Relief, sweet and dizzying, spiraled through her. She stood on tiptoes and pressed her mouth to his. "Thanks. So much."

She raced down the stairs to the front door. She pulled it open, her smile and exuberant greeting dying on her lips. Peter stood outside the door, but Becky was nowhere to be seen.

She fought the sudden panic that took her breath away. "Where's Rebecca?"

"Waiting in the car with Jeanne."

"In the car," she repeated, looking to the courtyard gate and beyond. "Why?"

"We need to talk."

She returned her gaze to him, noticing for the first time his determined eyes and set jaw. He looked ready to do battle.

Fear clutched at her, but she stiffened her spine and lifted her chin. "Is Rebecca all right?"

"She's fine, of course. I take very good care of her."

Meaning she didn't. Anger nudged at her distress. "Then I can't imagine what we have to say to each other."

"Can't you?" He edged around her and into her foyer, snapping the door shut behind himself.

She frowned, the blood beginning to pound in her head. "How dare you? This is my house."

"How dare you?" he countered. "Rebecca is my daughter."

"What's that supposed to mean? I've never questioned your rights or denied you—"

"Do you have something going on with Jack Jacobs?"

She took an involuntary step back, stunned. "Where did that come from?"

"Maybe from the side of every bus in southern California."

The publicity blitz. Again. "For heaven's sake, Peter. It's a publicity campaign for the show."

"It's an abomination. It's disgraceful."

She jerked up her chin, furious. "It's not. You act like the photos depict us having sex or something."

"That tag line—"

"Refers to whether or not we'll like the movies."

"Like hell." He faced her, his fists on his hips. "I've seen the show. There's a sexual thing between you two."

"You're completely irrational, Peter. When it comes to Jack, you always have been." She took a step toward him. "I want my daughter. And I want you to leave."

She turned toward the door and reached for the

knob. He caught her arm, his fingers digging into her flesh. "Are you sleeping with him?"

His grip hurt, and tears of pain stung her eyes. She fought them back, just as she fought to keep her alarm from showing—she saw something wild in her ex-husband's eyes, something she had never seen before. And it scared her. "Take your hand off me, Peter."

He tightened his grip instead; tomorrow, she knew, she would have bruises. "I don't want my daughter around him. I don't want him buying her stuffed animals." He shook her. "And I don't want to spend another weekend hearing 'Jack this and Jack that.'"

She wrenched her arm free. "Maybe I don't want Rebecca spending time with Jeanne."

"She's my wife."

"But once upon a time she was your girlfriend."

"You are sleeping with him."

Shaking with rage, she pointed toward the door. "Get out."

Instead he moved closer to her. "What do you suppose the judge is going to think about all this? You carrying on with the same man who—"

"You heard Jill. Get out."

They both swung in the direction of the stairs. Jack stood on the second to last step, his deep-blue eyes on Peter, the expression in them one of barely controlled fury. His fists were clenched at his sides, almost as tightly as his jaw. Jack would like nothing more than to punch her ex-husband squarely in the mouth. And as much as a part of her would like him to do just that, she knew it would be the worst thing he could do. She had to think of Rebecca.

She opened her mouth to say something—she wasn't sure what—but Peter beat her to it.

"You bastard." Peter took a step toward Jack, his face mottled with rage. "I ought to kill you."

"You could try." Jack swept his gaze arrogantly over the slighter man. "But it would seem like a bit of an overreaction to me. I don't believe we've ever even met."

"I was right all along." Peter looked at her accusingly. "You are sleeping with him."

Angry heat stung her cheeks. Anger at Peter's ridiculous obsession over her relationship with Jack, and Jack's presumptuous behavior. "We're colleagues, Peter. For heaven's sake, you're not going to start—"

"What if we are sleeping together?" Jack crossed to stand directly in front of the smaller man. Peter was forced to cock his head back to meet Jack's gaze. "You, obviously, are sleeping with someone else."

"She's my wife!"

"She wasn't always." Jack lowered his voice. "Exactly how long was it after you and Jill split up that you started seeing your new wife? Or did you start that while still married to Jill?"

Something passed over Peter's expression, a kind of panic, and her stomach turned. He had been unfaithful to her, she realized, shocked. Peter had started seeing Jeanne before they'd separated. And to think, she'd felt guilty.

"This is preposterous," Peter huffed. "Ridiculous."

"No more than what you're accusing us of." Jack lowered his voice. "And before you threaten Jill with 'what the judge is going to think,' maybe you should consider what he'll think of your own behavior?"

"You can't prove a thing, Jacobs."

"Neither can you." Jack jerked his head in the direction of the door. "Now, I believe Jill asked you to leave."

Jill pushed through the door before Peter, afraid he would try to leave with Rebecca. She needn't have worried; Peter stayed several paces behind her.

As soon as she saw her mother, Rebecca burst out of the car, all smiles. "Mommy!"

Jill laughed and held out her arms, joy cleansing her of the nastiness of the confrontation with Peter. Becky launched herself into Jill's arms. "I missed you, sweetheart," Jill said, hugging her daughter tightly. "So, so much."

"I missed you, too, Mommy."

Jill drew away so that she could see her daughter's face. "I saved you some pumpkin pie."

The little girl scrunched up her nose. "I like apple."

"I know." She smiled again and planted a kiss on her baby-soft cheek. "I saved you some of that too."

Peter set Rebecca's suitcase on the sidewalk beside them. "Got a good-bye hug for your daddy?"

Rebecca turned to her father and he scooped her up for a big hug. Jill shifted her gaze to Jeanne, waiting in the car. The other woman watched Peter; she looked near tears. Jill felt a ripple of pity for the woman who'd gotten caught in her and Peter's nasty battle.

After he and Rebecca had said their good-byes, Peter climbed into his car and drove off. Only then did Rebecca notice Jack standing in the doorway to the courtyard. She waved. "Hi, Jack. Did you bring me anything?"

"Becky!" Jill sent her daughter a disapproving glance.

Jack started toward them. "Not this time, sweetie." He took the suitcase from Jill's hands.

Becky's smile faded. "I lost my bear. We looked but couldn't find her."

Jill met Jack's gaze. Rebecca had taken the bear with her to her father's, and she hadn't a doubt where it had disappeared to. Or why. Anger filled her, and she saw the same emotion in Jack's eyes.

"That's okay." Jack ruffled Becky's hair. "I'll buy you another one."

The little girl brightened and chattered about her Thanksgiving all the way upstairs. When she ran to her room to check on her toys, Jack turned to Jill. "That ex-husband of yours has a problem. And I don't like the way he's involving Rebecca in it."

The tenuous hold she had on her emotions snapped, and she turned to Jack, so furious, she shook. "You don't like the way he's involving Rebecca? How do you think I feel? I'm her mother."

Jack frowned. "I'm sure you're upset and angry."

"And frightened." She clasped her hands together, struggling to keep her voice low so that Rebecca wouldn't hear. "You jeopardized my chances of gaining custody of Rebecca this afternoon. I asked you to stay out of sight while Peter was here, and instead you paraded down the stairs like some sort of macho hero."

Fury darkened his eyes. "Come on, Jill. Did you think I could stand back and let that jerk threaten and manhandle you?"

"He wasn't manhandling—"

"No? Then what are these?" Jack caught her arm, and she winced. Purple bruises were already appearing on her arm. "Maybe we should photograph this for the judge to see."

She sank into the couch. "He's never been like that before. He's always been a good father. When we were married, he was gentle." She brought her hands to her face for a moment, then dropped them. "But when it comes to you, he's so jealous. He always has been."

"It's crazy. The guy needs counseling."

She bit her lip. "It's not . . . completely crazy."

Jack stopped pacing and looked at her. "What do you mean?"

She took a deep breath, shame and regret balling up inside of her. She lowered her eyes to her hands, which were clasped in her lap. "During our marriage Peter accused me of not loving him as much as I loved you. He accused me of . . . still being in love with you. Of having married him on the rebound." She returned her gaze to Jack's. "He was right."

Jack made a strangled sound, but whether it was one of disbelief, surprise, or pain, she wasn't sure. She looked away. "I didn't go into the marriage knowing that. I only realized later. I never loved him as much as he deserved to be loved."

She cocked her chin up with false bravado. "So you see, he has a right to be angry. He divorced me, but he had good reason. And now I'm so afraid he's going to use that against me. I'm so afraid he's going to find a way to take Rebecca away from me. And a part of me—irrational though it is—feels like I brought this whole thing with Rebecca on myself."

Jack said nothing. He hadn't a clue how to feel, let alone what to say. Jill had still loved him while married to Peter? He could hardly fathom it. He understood her fear more, her mixed feelings over her ex-husband and the divorce. He wished he didn't—then he wouldn't hurt for her. He wouldn't feel responsible.

"Ah, Jilly . . ." Jack squatted down in front of her and took her hands. "You went into the marriage with good intentions; you tried to make it work. You can't feel guilty or blame yourself for something that wasn't your fault."

He brought her hands to his lips. "And you can't expect to be punished for a sin you didn't even commit. You're a good mother. You tried to be a good wife. That's all the judge is going to see."

Her eyes were heartbreakingly vulnerable. In that moment he wanted to hold and protect her, he wanted to spend the rest of his life reassuring her that everything was going to be all right.

"Jilly . . ." He touched her face, tracing it lightly with the tips of his fingers. "If you still loved me, why did you leave?"

"Because you didn't love me back," she whispered. "Because you couldn't give me what I wanted . . . what I needed. A commitment. A forever."

In that instant, as he'd searched for something to say, Rebecca had burst back into the room, shattering the moment. He'd instantly come to his senses, and gotten out of there as fast as he could, but he'd been unable to put the way she'd looked at him—and the way that look made him feel—out of his mind.

Jack pulled into his driveway and cut off the car's engine. He was in too far, too deep. He looked at Jill and felt his heart being wrenched from his chest. He looked at Rebecca and felt a kind of tenderness, an involvement, he had no business feeling. He wasn't Rebecca's father, brother, or uncle, so why did he find himself caring so much about what happened to her?

He climbed out of his car and went inside. He walked to the kitchen, fished a beer out of the refrigerator, popped the top, and crossed to the sink and looked out the window above it. He set the beverage down untouched, his thoughts filled with his father, filled with visual remembrances, as crisp and clear as if the events had happened yesterday instead of years ago.

He remembered his father coming home from the factory every night at a quarter past five. He'd come home silent and grim, his mouth thin and his hands calloused and cut from hours of working the machines. His routine never changed. Without a word of greeting to any of them, he would enter the house and retreat to the living room, where his saxophone was displayed, set up in a corner like an altar to lost dreams. Sometimes he would gaze at the instrument until the room would become too dark for him to do so any longer. Jack had felt his unhappiness, his dissatisfaction, so keenly, he had ached with it.

"You did this to me," he had told Jack on many occasions. *"You, your mother, and the rest. Stay single and stay free, unless you want to end up like your old man."*

His old man.

Jack gazed at his reflection in the window, searching, as he had countless times before, for any hint of a resemblance to his father. He'd spent his life trying not to be like him. He'd made every decision, taken every turn in the road to lead him away from his father's life, away from that terrible threat.

Jill had still loved him when she'd married Peter. He

sucked in a sharp breath. She'd walked out because he couldn't give her what she needed and wanted.

He still couldn't.

He fisted his fingers against the cool, rigid glass. What had he been doing this weekend? How could he have knowingly involved them in something that was so wrong for them both? Something that in the end would make them both unhappy.

He muttered an oath. Because when he was with Jill, he forgot vows about staying unattached. He forgot about the ugliness of life, forgot about his fears for the future. With Jill he saw nothing but her, felt nothing but . . . happy.

The phone rang. It was Sue.

"Dad's sick," she said without preamble.

Jack felt her words like a punch to his gut. "What?"

"You heard me, Dad's sick." She made a sound of frustration and disgust. "He hasn't been to the doctor, but he doesn't look good and has zero energy."

Jack rubbed his eyes, his pulse pounding in his head. "He refuses to go to the doctor? What's his deal? Would he rather sit in front of his shrine in the living room and die?"

"Basically."

After a moment Jack swore. "The man's mean, you know that? He's stubborn, unreasonable, and a major pain in the ass."

"True." Sue cleared her throat. "I think you should come see him."

"We went through this the other day. I thought—"

"I'm worried about you."

"About me?" Jack scowled. "What the hell for?"

"I'm worried about how you're going to feel if Dad

dies and you haven't made your peace with him. Think about it, Jack."

They talked for a few minutes more before Jack hung up the phone, his head spinning.

His father die? Could he really be so ill?

Jack drew in a shaky breath, a dozen different, conflicting emotions barreling through him. *How would he feel if his father died and he hadn't tried to make his peace with him?*

He didn't know. Jack drew his eyebrows together. He just didn't know.

NINE

"You're okay about Jack watching you while I meet with my editor?" Jill stopped at the red light and turned to her daughter.

"Uh-huh." Rebecca pulled the lollipop out of her mouth and smiled at her. "I like it when Jack watches me. I get to do whatever I want."

"Mmm." Jill rolled her eyes and shifted her gaze back to the road. In the weeks since Thanksgiving Jack had spent a good bit of time with Rebecca. Christmas had come and gone, the New Year, Valentine's Day. He had seemed genuinely to enjoy her daughter. He never balked at the idea of children's activities or at getting down on the floor to play, and it showed in how crazy Rebecca was about him. And yet Jill felt that Jack held himself from Rebecca. From really getting to know her, from getting emotionally involved with her.

"Maybe he'll take me to Chuckie Cheese."

The light changed, and Jill started through the intersection. "I don't think so, honey. I'm going to be only about an hour."

"Oh." Rebecca slumped back into her seat, her expression devastated.

"Maybe we can go later."

"Maybe."

"Besides, you brought all your favorite games to play."

Rebecca brightened and twisted in her seat to look at the stack of games on the floor in back. "I want to play Mousetrap first."

Jill accelerated to pass the car creeping along in front of her, then eased back into the right lane. "I'm sure that will be fine with Jack."

Rebecca drew her eyebrows together into a thoughtful frown. "Mom?"

"Hmm?"

"Does Jack like me?"

The question took Jill by surprise. She shot her daughter a startled glance, then turned her attention back to the road. "Very much, sweetie. What made you ask that?"

For a few moments Rebecca said nothing, then she shrugged. "He didn't come to my pageant."

Jill gripped the steering wheel, remembering that afternoon, her own anger, Rebecca's hurt. They'd been all set to go to Rebecca's preschool Christmas pageant, and Jack had called and begged off. He'd had a last minute review to do, he'd told her. His editor had called.

That hadn't been it at all. She'd heard the distance in his voice. *The wall.* In the weeks since she and Jack had become lovers, the wall, as she'd come to think of it, had come and gone. One day everything would be going great between them, so well that her heart would swell and her hopes rise. Then *the wall* would come crashing down. And suddenly she could get closer to an electric fence than she could to Jack.

It had become so predictable, she'd come to expect it.

She reached across the seat and squeezed her daughter's hand. "He couldn't. He had to work. He told you how sorry he was."

The little girl's chin shot up. "Daddy would have come no matter what."

That hurt, as did the fact she had to remind her daughter of. "But Jack's not your daddy."

She stopped at the light and looked at her daughter. Rebecca's chin was quivering and her eyes were bright. A lump formed in Jill's throat. She hadn't wanted her relationship with Jack to hurt Rebecca, had promised herself that it wouldn't. She saw now that it had. By Jill's becoming involved with Jack, her daughter had become involved with him too.

She hadn't understood that before, not really. But then, since her divorce she hadn't seen anyone else except for an occasional date. A horn blared behind her, and she jerked her eyes and attention back to the road. The light had turned green, and she moved through the intersection.

"Mom?"

"Yes, sweetie?"

"I have two mommies. You and Mommy Jeanne."

She suspected where her daughter was heading, and she wished she was wrong. She took a deep breath, preparing herself.

"Can I have two daddies too?"

She swallowed. "Sure, baby."

"Jack doesn't want to be my other daddy."

Jill glanced at Rebecca in surprise. She'd been wrong. She'd prepared herself for her daughter to ask if Jack could be her father. But this . . . Jill bit her lip, working to hold back the hurt, fighting to keep her own emotions from showing. "Why do you say that, honey?"

Rebecca shrugged, and reached into her bag to fish out a toy. Jill let the subject drop. She already knew why her daughter felt that way. Rebecca felt Jack's distance the same as she did. And it hurt Rebecca. Why hadn't she seen that before today? How could she have been so blind?

She flexed her fingers on the steering wheel. Because, when it came to Jack, she had always been blind. She'd spent every available minute with him, head-over-heels in love and immersed in their dizzying affair, and time had flown carelessly by.

She thought of those weeks together. Their lovemaking had been at once passionate and tender, desperate and languorous. They'd laughed and talked, spent time alone and with Rebecca. They'd fallen into a steady rhythm of doing *Reel Reviews*, and the show had continued to be a hit.

Except for those times when *the wall* had come crashing down between them, it had been wonderful having Jack back in her life. Fun. Fulfilling.

It had been easy to allow herself to fantasize what it would be like to be a family, the three of them. It had been easy to fantasize that he loved her, that he wanted to be a father to Rebecca.

A fantasy was all it was.

She drew in a steadying breath. Jack had said nothing of love to her, hadn't spoken of the future, had never referred to himself as a father figure for Rebecca. He never would.

Rebecca saw that clearly, and she was only five years old.

She drew in a deep breath, her chest hurting. What had she expected? She knew going into this thing that he didn't love her, that he never would. She had convinced herself that it didn't matter, had convinced herself that his feelings for her would grow and deepen.

She had convinced herself that they had a real chance at happiness, at a future together.

She'd been a starry-eyed fool. They were the same people they'd been five years before, the same people having the same doomed relationship. She had to get out of this before it destroyed her. Before Rebecca grew to love and depend on Jack.

Heart pounding, she turned onto Jack's street. But she didn't want to let him go. She didn't want to say good-bye, didn't have the strength of will. She loved him.

"There's Jack!" Rebecca squealed. "Look, Mommy!"

He stood on the front porch, waiting for them, tall and strong and breathtakingly handsome. He wore a cream-colored cable-knit sweater and a pair of faded Levis; his hair looked damp, his face freshly shaven. He smiled and waved as he saw her car.

Her stomach turned over. She loved him so damn much, she ached.

They weren't the same people they had been five years ago, she thought. Jack had changed. Five years ago he'd shared nothing of himself with her; this time he had opened himself and his heart.

Time, she thought, turning into his drive. He just needed more time.

He started down the steps, reaching the driveway just as she pulled the car to a stop. He opened Rebecca's door, and the little girl tumbled out. "Jack! Jack! Look what I brought for us to play."

She went to the rear car door and struggled to open it. She finally did, and scrambled inside, knocking the stack of games over. Jack laughed. "Oh, boy, Mousetrap."

"She wants to play that one first," Jill said, coming around the side of the car.

Jack caught her to him, lowering his mouth to hers in a quick, fierce kiss, holding her tightly for a moment longer than usual. When he released her, she met his eyes. Something about his expression tugged at her heartstrings. He looked sad and a little lost. She reached up and lightly stroked his cheek. "Is everything all right?"

"Fine."

His lips curved into an automatic smile, but the smile, she saw, didn't reach his eyes. She drew her eyebrows together, concerned. "Are you up to watching Becky? If not, I could call Margaret."

"No way. Becky and I are going to have a great time." He swung toward the car and the little girl rummaging in the backseat. "Right, Rebecca?"

"Right," she called.

Even as she opened her mouth to question him more, she realized what had happened, and her heart sank. *The wall.* Erected and fixed firmly in place. She turned away from him to help Rebecca, disappointment bitter on her tongue. This morning when she'd talked to him, everything had been great. What had happened between then and now to cause him to distance himself from her?

After collecting the stack of games, they started for the house, Rebecca chattering and Jack silent. As soon as they stepped inside, Rebecca hugged Jill good-bye and raced off in search of Jack's new kitten, leaving her and Jack alone in the foyer.

Jill folded her arms across her aching chest, a feeling of hopelessness washing over her. "Well, I guess I'd better be going."

Jack looked at her, then away, obviously lost in his own thoughts. "I suppose."

She took a deep breath. "Jack?"

He met her eyes. "Yeah?"

"Are you sure you don't mind baby-sitting?"

"Yeah. I'm sure."

Jill caught her bottom lip between her teeth, turned to leave. She had the sense he wanted to say something to her, that he needed something from her. She called herself a fool.

When she reached the door, she stopped and met his eyes. "I'll be about an hour, hour and a half tops. If you need anything, you can reach me at the paper."

"No problem."

She started through the door, and he caught her hand. "Jilly?"

She stopped and turned toward him. "Yes?"

For a moment she thought he would say nothing. Then he pulled her into his arms and held her, his face pressed against her hair, his arms curved tightly around her. She felt a desperation in the way he clung to her, a need. He hugged her as if he feared she was going to disappear.

She put her arms around him, returning his grip, feeling closer to him than she had since Thanksgiving morning when he'd told her about his father and his past.

Moments passed. From the kitchen she heard Rebecca trying to coax the kitten from its hiding place; from outside came the sound of a group of rowdy teenagers.

Jack relaxed his hold on her. She tipped her head back and met his eyes, filled with pain—naked, raw. A second later it was gone.

"Jack?" she whispered, a shudder of fear moving through her. "Is everything all right?"

He released her and forced a stiff smile. "Everything's fine."

She frowned, obviously unconvinced. "Does something have to be wrong for me to hold you?" He took a step toward her. "I must not be doing it enough. I think I'll need to remedy that situation, and soon."

She drew a quick breath, relieved. "Oh, you think so?"

He leaned a fraction of an inch closer; his breath stirred against her cheek. "Uh-huh. I like holding you, Ms. Lansing. In fact there are other things I like doing with you as well. Things I like very much."

He slid his hands to the small of her back, holding them there for one tantalizing moment, then moving them lower. He leaned closer, trailing his lips over the curve of her cheek to the shell of her ear. "Perhaps tonight," he whispered, "I can detail just what those things are."

Heat washed over her, and her pulse began to thrum. "Tonight," she repeated, swaying against him.

He laughed softly, then nipped her earlobe. "But for now I bet your editor wonders where you are."

For one moment Jack's words didn't register. When they did, she sprang away from him, checked her watch, and groaned. "Rob hates it when I'm late! He considers tardiness a major character flaw."

She stood on tiptoe, pressed a quick kiss on his lips, called another good-bye to Rebecca, then raced out the front door and across the front porch.

Jack watched her go, his smile fading, sadness settling over him like a heavy blanket. Jill backed out of his drive, then roared down the street, and he turned away from the door.

Dying. His father was dying.

How could it be true?

He pressed the heels of his hands to his eyes. He would have liked to have told Jill; it would have been nice to have someone to share his feelings with, to lean on, if only for the moment.

He wasn't a man who leaned. He wasn't a man who asked for emotional support. He managed alone. Always. One exception could lead to another, then another. As it was, he had already become too accustomed to Jill's smile and laugh, her warmth.

From the kitchen came the sound of little-girl giggles. A smile tugged involuntarily at his mouth. He'd grown too attached to Rebecca as well. He found himself looking forward to her playful antics, her sweet, trusting ways. Sometimes when she looked at him, he felt ten feet tall and able to conquer the world.

His head filled with thoughts of his father, and pain

twisted in his gut. *"Love,"* his father had sneered on many an occasion. *"It'll snare you, boy. Then squeeze the life out of you."*

Jack ran his fingers through his hair. Had his father ever loved the woman he had married? Had he ever been so besotted, he'd been unable to imagine an hour without her, let alone a lifetime? And had he ever loved his children, had he ever looked at them and felt ten feet tall?

He didn't know, not for sure. But if he hadn't, why had he married Sally Jacobs? Why had he stayed with his wife and children instead of taking off, the way a lot of men did?

Jack massaged the back of his neck, working the knotted muscles, his eyebrows drawn together in thought. Sue had called not even an hour ago. Cancer, she'd said. Their father had it everywhere.

A dozen different emotions moved through him. Grief and despair. Shock. And an overwhelming confusion, about his feelings, about what he should do, what he needed to do.

"Jack?" Rebecca tugged on his sleeve. "Can we play Mousetrap now?"

Jack looked at her, realizing he stood in the middle of the foyer, front door open behind him, gazing at nothing. He hadn't even realized she'd given up on the kitten and come looking for him.

"Sure." He tried to smile but failed miserably. She cocked her head, her eyes full of questions.

He turned away from her bright, inquisitive face, collected the game, and swung the front door shut. They went to the living room, sat on the floor, and Jack began putting the game's contraption together. They never played by the rules. He simply put together the elaborate trap, and she set it into motion, over and over.

But usually she chattered while he assembled it, usually she giggled and told stories or tried to help him. Today she was silent.

He shot a quick glance at her and found her looking at him, chin on fist, brow furrowed. "Do you want to play?"

She nodded, but didn't take her gaze from his. He returned his attention to the board and to building the trap.

"What's the matter?"

He met her eyes, then lowered his to the game board again. "Not a thing, cutie."

"You look sad."

He looked at her once more. "Sad?"

"The way Mommy does when Daddy comes to pick me up. When she tells me good-bye." Rebecca pursed her lips. "Who did you say good-bye to today?"

Emotion choked him. *Good-bye.* He'd never said good-bye to his father. Now he may never have the chance.

"My father's sick," he said softly, roughly. "And I'm . . . it's hard to—"

His throat closed over the words, and she slipped her hand into his, curling her small fingers around his bigger ones. "Is he real sick?"

"Yes," Jack managed.

The child was quiet a moment, as if thinking about that. She scooted closer to him and rested her head on his arm. "When I'm real sick, my mommy sits by my bed all night."

Tears burned the back of his eyes, and he blinked against them, calling himself a fool. "Does she?"

"An' she gives me ice cream. It makes me feel better."

He ran his hand over Rebecca's silky-soft hair, touched by her sweetness. By her childlike ability to unself-consciously share herself and her feelings.

What would it be like to be so open and trusting? he wondered, smoothing his hand over her hair once more. What would it be like to have no fear about the future?

"She's a nice mommy," he murmured.

Rebecca made a small sound of contentment. "If she were sick, I'd sit by her bed all night."

Jack smiled and dropped a light kiss on the top of her head. "And give her ice cream?"

She nodded. " 'Course. I love my mommy best of all."

They played Mousetrap then, and about a dozen other games afterward. Even as they laughed and joked, he turned what Rebecca had said to him over in his head. Something in her words tugged at him. But for the life of him, he couldn't figure out what it was.

Jack took his eyes from the road to glance at Jill, sitting beside him in the car. She sat ramrod straight in the seat, hands clasped in her lap, face turned to the side window. Even as stiff and in control as she looked, he saw that she was ready to fall apart. Her skin was pale, the line of her mouth achingly vulnerable, her eyes bright with unshed tears.

She was frightened. Of the future. Of losing her daughter.

He swallowed hard and returned his attention to the road. They'd just come from a meeting with her lawyer, the last before the custody hearing next week. He hadn't wanted to go, had known he was already too emotionally involved, but he had been unable to refuse her.

The attorney had gone over how the hearing would unfold, what kind of questions to expect from the judge and Peter's lawyer, and he had discussed frankly what he thought her chances were and why.

The lawyer thought her chances were good. That was the good news. The bad news they'd already known —there was a chance the judge could rule in favor of Peter.

He drew his eyebrows together and tightened his fingers on the steering wheel. Sitting through the meeting had been a nightmare. He'd seen, had actually felt, Jill's fear. And he'd been helpless to reassure her. He'd felt as if murmuring one soft word or giving her a single comforting touch would have sent him tumbling over the edge of some invisible cliff and into an abyss of emotion. An abyss he would never escape from.

So he'd remained cool and in control; he'd asked pointed, deliberate questions. He had hoped that later, when she was being consumed by fear and uncertainty, he would be able to reassure her with facts.

All the while he'd wanted to hit the lawyer just for standing there and calmly telling Jill that she might lose Rebecca. He'd wanted to take a drive down the freeway, find Peter Knight, and pound him until he admitted he was a spineless jerk and promised to leave Jill and Rebecca alone.

"What if I lose her?" Jill whispered suddenly, turning toward him, her face ashen.

Jack flexed his fingers on the steering wheel. "It's not going to happen."

She lowered her eyes to her clasped hands. "You're one hundred percent certain of that?" He hesitated a moment, and she made a sound of pain. "At least you don't lie to me."

He muttered an oath and stopped as the light up ahead turned red. "I can't claim being one hundred percent certain the judge will grant you custody, but I will claim being ninety-five percent certain."

"Really?"

The look in her eyes was so hopeful, it hurt. He sucked in a deep breath. "Yes, really. As your lawyer said, it helps that Rebecca's a girl, not a boy. That Peter has another child now, also a daughter, counts in your favor."

The light changed, and he started through the intersection. "And didn't he assure you that Peter's threats about our relationship and your association with *Reel Reviews* were nothing more than hot air? All the judge cares about is what kind of parents you are. Period."

"Peter is a good father." She twisted her fingers together. "He loves Rebecca as much as any father ever loved a daughter. And that scares me. The judge will see that, he'll listen to Jeanne's testimony to that fact; he'll listen to Peter's mother effuse the same thing. And who will I have to tell what a wonderful mother I am? Rebecca's preschool teacher? Her baby-sitter?"

She made a small, choked sound, and Jack saw how she worked to keep it together. "Peter's lawyer is going to play heavily on the fact that I work, that Peter can offer Rebecca a traditional family life, complete with a dog, a sibling, and a neighborhood full of kids. I can't give her that."

Jack grimaced. That had been the downside. The lawyer had been brutally honest about the things in Jill's favor, and the things that weren't.

He hesitated, not wanting to reveal his own uncertainty. "Don't borrow trouble, Jilly. Don't worry about this more than you have to. It's only going to make it worse."

She bit her lip and looked away, letting the subject drop. He followed her lead, knowing he wasn't helping, understanding that now was not the time to try to reason with her. Her emotions were too raw.

And so were his.

His father had been right, Jack thought grimly. You couldn't have it all: love and a family, a smashing career. Something suffered, someone got hurt, even if only the person juggling all the balls. He'd seen the truth of his father's words before today, but he had tried to fight the truth, had wanted to more than anything, because of the way he felt about Jill and Rebecca.

They reached the condo, and without waiting for him, she climbed out of the car and started quickly for the front gate, almost running. He followed her, wondering at her haste. He understood the moment Jill caught sight of Rebecca. He'd forgotten that she'd returned from seeing her father that afternoon. Jill's face lit up, and she swept the child into her arms.

"I missed you, baby. So much."

"Me, too." Rebecca returned her mother's fierce hug, her eyes squeezed tight shut.

"Did you have a good time with Margaret?"

"Uh-huh." The little girl smiled and squirmed out of Jill's arms. "We made something for you."

"Right here, Poppet." Margaret walked into the room, carrying a plate of cookies. She handed it to Rebecca, who in turn proudly displayed the misshapen sugar cookies.

"They look great," Jack murmured, studying the offering.

"Yummy," Jill echoed.

"Have one," Rebecca said, beaming. "They're for you and Mommy."

The phone rang, and after taking a cookie, Jill went to the other room to answer it.

It was Dana. "Jill, you're home." She heard the relief in her friend's voice, and a wave of gratitude moved over her. Dana had proved herself a real friend over the past weeks; she'd been supportive, helpful, and as steady as a rock. "How'd it go?"

"It went okay. Just as I expected anyway. We just walked in."

Dana made a sound of distress. "I was hoping for some kind of miracle, like maybe Peter would come to his senses and call this whole thing off."

Jill twisted the phone cord around her index finger. "No such luck, I'm afraid."

"I'm really sorry, Jill. And if you need anything at all, don't hesitate to call. Tell Jack the same goes for him."

Jill drew her eyebrows together. "For Jack? What do you mean?"

"You know, because of his dad's illness. I know how hard he must be taking it."

Jill looked to the doorway of the other room, catching a glimpse of Jack and Rebecca. He was squatting down in front of her daughter, munching on a cookie and listening raptly to something she was saying.

Jack's father was ill? When had Jack learned that?

"Jill? Are you there?"

"Yes, I'm here." She cleared her throat. "Jack hasn't mentioned his father being sick. Is it serious?"

Dana said nothing for a moment, then swore softly. "He has cancer. It's really bad."

The cookie slipped from her fingers, splintering into a half-dozen pieces as it hit the wooden floor. "Cancer? Are you sure?"

"It's everywhere, Jill. The doctors don't give him much hope."

Dying, Jill thought, her heart going out to Jack. How awful for him. He must feel terrible, especially considering his and his father's strained relationship.

But he hadn't told her.

Jill bent to retrieve the cookie, her hands trembling so badly, she could hardly collect the pieces. How could he not have told her? she wondered, stunned. How could he have kept something so important from her? They were lovers. They were supposed to share everything.

Hurt and betrayal spiraled through her. But Jack had shared nothing with her.

Dana cleared her throat. "Look, Jill, I'm sorry, I shouldn't have said any—"

"No, Dana, it's not you who should be apologizing."

"He only told me because he thought he might need some time off."

"I understand, Dana. You don't have to explain anything to me." Jill drew in a deep breath. "Thanks for calling, I really appreciate it. I'll call you later."

She dropped the receiver into its cradle, then stared blindly at it, fighting the swell of emotions that threatened to drown her. Hurt and wounded pride. Anger and despair. Sympathy for Jack.

What a blind fool she had been, what a naive idiot. Thanksgiving morning he'd shared himself with her. He'd told her about his past, his father, his feelings. And she'd held tightly to that, holding it out to herself and her heart as a symbol of hope for their relationship and a sign that there was a chance for them.

She'd been so wrong.

They were no closer than they had been five years before. He was the same man, she the same woman. And they were having the same doomed relationship.

She clenched her fingers, the bits of cookie crumbling in her hand. Jack hadn't wanted to come with her today; she had seen it in his eyes even as he'd agreed to accompany her. She wished now that she hadn't even asked him. She'd wanted his moral support, had wanted someone who could shore her up if she started to fall apart.

Tears stung her eyes. She'd wanted him to reassure her that everything would be all right. Had wanted him to promise that he would be there for her, no matter what.

Just as she now wanted to be there for him. She wanted to hold him and reassure him. She wanted to be by his side through good and bad. He wouldn't allow her to do that. Just as today at the lawyer's office he hadn't been able to give her what she needed.

Jack kept himself from her in so many ways.

The wall he'd erected the day he'd baby-sat for Rebecca two weeks earlier hadn't come down, not once.

Even when they'd made love. She lowered her eyes. The bits of cookie were scattered on the floor by her feet, alone and broken. It didn't take a rocket scientist to figure out what was going on—he'd ended the relationship already. He was waiting until after the hearing to make it official.

The tears that had flooded her eyes, brimmed, threatening to fall. She straightened her spine and started for Jack. She'd known this would happen from the beginning; there was no reason for tears or hysterics now. He didn't love her. He never had. Plain and simple.

Jill pushed impatiently at the tears that escaped and rolled down her cheek. She couldn't go on this way. If Jack couldn't give her his heart, if he couldn't give her everything, she would have to tell him good-bye.

"Margaret?" She drew in a deep breath. "Could you stay a little longer? I need to talk with Jack."

"Sure." The woman looked from her to Jack, her brows lowered in question. "Becky and I could go down to the courtyard to see the fish."

"Thank you. We'll be down in a few minutes."

After she heard the front door shut, she turned to Jack. "That was Dana," she said softly. "She told me your father's sick."

Jack's expression tightened. "He is."

"I'm sorry." She slipped her shaking hands into her trouser pockets. "When did you learn he was ill?"

"A couple of weeks ago. The day I sat for Rebecca."

The truth of that ricocheted painfully through her. She realized she'd wanted him to come up with some wild, harebrained excuse for not having told her. She couldn't fool herself about what he felt for her, not any longer. "Is there anything I can do?"

The closed expression in his eyes tore at her. "Thanks, Jilly, but I have to deal with this alone."

She felt as if he had slapped her. "But you don't have to deal with it alone. Don't you get it, Jack? It's okay for you to lean on me, it's okay to need me."

He said nothing and she swung away from him, needing a moment to compose herself and her thoughts. After she had, she faced him once more. "Why didn't you tell me?"

This time it was Jack who turned from her. For a long time he said nothing, then he shook his head. "I don't know."

Another sterling response. She made a sound of pain. "What are we doing here? What do you want from this relationship?"

His hunted expression clawed at her. He had looked at her that way once before—the day she'd told him she was pregnant. She shook her head and took a step back from him. "We don't want the same things out of this, out of us. We didn't five years ago, and we still don't."

"I don't want to lose you, Jilly. I lost you once, and I don't want to again."

"So marry me," she said softly, crossing to him. She lifted a hand to his cheek. "If you don't want to lose me, marry me. Be a father to Rebecca. She loves you already."

He covered her hand with his own. "Don't do this, Jilly. Not now."

"Then when? Next week, next year? Ten years from now? Life's too short to throw away on a useless situation."

"Is that what this has been? Useless?" He brought

her fingers to his lips. "That's not the way it's felt to me."

She gazed into his eyes, her heart breaking. "But you're not the one who wanted something impossible from the relationship. You're not the one who had to face that impossibility every day."

He dropped her hand and crossed to the window that looked over the courtyard. Below, Rebecca played. He watched her chase the neighbor's cat; he imagined he could hear her laughter. She stopped suddenly, as if sensing his scrutiny, and looked up. She saw him, grinned and waved, and his heart turned over. What would Rebecca think when he stopped coming around? Would she think he didn't like her anymore?

He turned to face Jill again, frustration balling in his gut. "Why did you get involved with me again, knowing what you did about me and your own needs?"

"I could ask you the same question."

He tipped his face up to the ceiling, his eyebrows drawn together. He thought of his father, the father of his childhood, brooding and bitter, unhappy; and he thought of his father now, sick, dying.

"Love, if it catches you, it'll squeeze the life out of you."

"You want to end up like me, boy?"

Jack struggled for even footing and a clear head, emotion welling inside him, making both impossible. He didn't want to end up like his father; he'd vowed he wouldn't. And yet . . .

He looked at Jill. The last months had been wonderful, too good to be true. But what came after that? How did he throw away everything he'd ever known about himself and his needs?

He expelled a long breath. "I got involved with you

again because I . . . because I can't resist you. I've never been able to."

Tears flooded her eyes. "And I love you. Sums up our relationship, past and present. Sad, isn't it?"

"Jilly . . . I'm sorry. I never wanted to hurt you. And I wish—"

She held up a hand, stopping him. "Don't make promises you can't keep or excuses for why you don't love me. It hurts when you do."

He crossed the room to her and cupped her face in his palms. Her cheeks were wet with her tears. "Let's not give up on this yet. When I said I didn't want to lose you, I meant it. We can compromise, find a solution that—"

"How do you compromise on love and commitment?" She covered his hands with her own. "You can't, Jack." She squeezed his fingers, then took a step away from him. "And I can't go on this way," she said softly, her voice thick. "It has to be everything or nothing."

He laughed, the sound angry and harsh even to his own ears. "I get it. Same old story, same old Jill. It has to be all your way or you walk. No compromise, no settling. You have to call all the shots."

She took a step back from him, looking stricken. She folded her arms protectively over herself. "That's not fair. We're not talking about a business negotiation here"—she pressed a hand to her chest—"we're talking about a relationship, we're talking about love and commitment."

"Not fair? Five years ago you did the exact same thing you're doing now." He swore. "You walked because I couldn't give you 'everything.' What about what

I could give you? What about what I did give you? Isn't that worth anything?"

He took a step toward her, hand out. "If what I'm telling you isn't true, then what the hell are you doing? And why are you doing it?"

She cocked up her chin. "Saving myself from being hurt. Saving myself months or even years of wishing for something that will never happen. Saving Rebecca from the same thing."

He shook his head. "Leave Rebecca out of this; this has to do with you. You're running away. Again."

"Look who's talking?" she shot back, her voice thick with emotion. "You're the one who's running away. And don't kid yourself, this has a lot to do with Rebecca. She picks up everything we're feeling, everything you're feeling. The way you emotionally distance yourself from her. From me."

He opened his mouth to deny her words, and she held up a hand, stopping him. "She asked me if I thought you liked her. She asked me why you didn't want to be her other daddy. Your indifference hurts her."

Jack took an involuntary step back, shocked. He thought of his father's apathy, his indifference, and of how much he had longed for his father's love. And how much not getting it had hurt.

Could he have hurt Rebecca that way?

"When?" he asked, his voice tight. "When did she say that?"

"A couple of weeks ago." Jill shook her head. "But it doesn't really matter when."

Jack swore and dragged his hands through his hair.

"I didn't want to hurt her. I just didn't want her to become too attached to me."

"Or was it that you didn't want to become too attached to her? Or to me?" She crossed to him and tipped her face up to his. "I love you, Jack. But I can't go on this way. I need you to love me."

Emotion threatened to swallow him, and he fought it. He cupped her face in his hands. "You had such a loveless childhood that if someone's not able to assure you of a perfect love, you run scared. You're afraid of being rejected, Jilly."

She pressed her hands against his chest, curling them into the weave of his pullover. "And what are you scared of, Jack? Being loved?"

He tightened his fingers. "I can't change the way I feel."

"Neither can I."

He moved his fingers gently across her cheeks, savoring the feel of her skin against his fingers, pain a living thing inside him. "So, where do we go from here?"

Her tears brimmed, spilling slowly over, rolling between his fingers. "You tell me, Jack. I don't want this to be good-bye."

He opened his mouth to try to reason with her, to somehow reassure her, then closed it, knowing they'd come to an impossible impasse. He bent and pressed his mouth to hers, tasting her tears, wondering if she tasted his regret, his sorrow.

Feeling as if he'd been ripped into a dozen ragged and bleeding pieces, he dropped his hands, turned, and walked away.

TEN

Jack pulled his rental car into the driveway of the two-story frame house, stopping the car but making no move to get out. Six years, he thought, moving his gaze over the structure. It had been six years since he'd sat, just as he was now, gazing at the place he'd once called home.

He narrowed his eyes, studying it. The house had been painted recently, a soft yellow replacing the white of years ago. The oak tree in the front yard seemed to have tripled in size, huge compared with the tree he'd climbed as a young boy. Its branches now stretched into the sky, covered with buds that would in a matter of weeks burst into leaves. Other than that, the place had changed little.

It felt good to be here, he thought, surprised, swinging the car door open and stepping out. He slammed the door shut behind him, then leaned against it. But then, anyplace, anything, would feel better than the past days had.

They'd been hell.

He rubbed his hand along the side of his cheek,

rough with a couple of days' growth of beard. As painful as it was to admit, he and Jill were through. He couldn't give her what she needed and deserved: love and commitment, a traditional family.

But he missed her. So much, he thought he might go crazy. He'd been such a bear that even the most good-natured of his acquaintances had thrown up their hands in disgust and ordered him to get a grip.

So he'd come home. To see his father and finally to lay the past to rest. And maybe, if there were any to be had, to get answers.

The curtain in the front window moved, and a small face peered out at him. Shaun, he thought, smiling, lifting his hand in greeting. The little boy's mouth dropped in surprise, and the curtain slipped back into place.

Jack grinned, wondering if the youngster had recognized him or if he was now excitedly reporting the presence of a stranger in the driveway. He hadn't called to tell anyone he was coming. He wasn't sure why, but he hadn't wanted his father to know.

He started for the house just as the front door burst open. Sue ran through, followed by his mother, Bonnie, and the twins. If family tradition had held through all these years, he'd arrived during the middle of the Sunday-afternoon meal.

"Jack!" The chorus resounded from one to another, and within seconds he was being hugged, tugged, and slapped on the back.

"You're home at last," his mother said, tears in her eyes.

"Why didn't you call?" Sue frowned. "I could have picked you up at the airport."

"Did you bring us anything, Uncle Jack?"

"Boys! Your manners!" Bonnie looked at him apologetically. "Welcome home, Jack."

Laughing, Jack answered each question in turn, letting himself be herded into the house. His mother insisted he eat, and they set a place for him at the table.

Home. He looked around the room, taking in the faded flower-print wallpaper, the mahogany buffet that had been his grandmother's, the china that had come from a catalog. Everything called to his memory, even the food his mother served. The stewed chicken with dumplings, the green beans cooked with too much fat to be politically correct, the home-baked apple crisp. As he ate, he recalled specific events of his childhood, including secretly feeding his beans to the dog under the table.

His sisters laughed as he recounted it. His mother clucked her tongue. "It didn't take your father long to figure out what was going on and chain the dog up outside during meals."

"Yeah, Jack," Sue chimed in. "You were lucky he didn't chain you up outside. He was so mad."

Everybody laughed again, and Jack made a face. "I think I would have preferred it over eating my own vegetables. For months afterward he made me eat two helpings to make up for the ones I hadn't eaten."

The conversation faltered, and Jack had the sense that they were all lost in their own childhood memories and with thoughts of Billy Jacobs.

He cleared his throat and tossed his napkin onto the table. "Where is Dad? The hospital?"

"Upstairs sleeping." Bonnie stood and began clearing the table, her expression grim with disapproval. "He refused to stay in the hospital."

"Against his doctor's wishes," Sue added, following

Bonnie to her feet. "They offered him little except to prolong his life, and I could understand his wanting to be home if he wanted to be near his family. But all he wants is to be left alone."

"The twins are sure he hates them." Bonnie lifted the stacked dinner plates. "Honestly, you'd think he'd want to get to know them a little before he dies."

Same as always, Jack thought. Terminally ill and his father still had no use for them.

"Girls, please," their mother murmured, her voice shaking. "Your father has very little time left. If he wants to spend it alone, then that should be his privilege."

Bonnie looked at him and rolled her eyes. Sue squeezed her mother's shoulder sympathetically. Jack realized that his sisters were here out of concern and love for their mother, not for Billy Jacobs.

But in their way his sisters had already made their peace with the old man, by being here, by being one of the family, day in and day out. He hadn't.

The time had come.

Jack took a deep breath and pushed himself away from the table. No matter how his father felt about him, he had to see him, had to face his past. Even if a big part of him didn't want to do either.

"Is it okay if I go up?"

His mother nodded, and Jack, aware of the rest of the family's eyes on him, left the dining room. They understood that he needed time alone with his father. He appreciated their sensitivity, although this meeting would have been easier with others present. He would have had a diversion that allowed him time to become accustomed to seeing his father again, to seeing him so ill. It would have given him a chance to hide his uncertainty. His despair.

He climbed the stairs, going without hesitation to his parents' bedroom door, transformed now into his father's sick room. It stood partially open, and he drew himself up, acknowledging that walking through this door was the last thing he wanted to do.

And the only thing he wanted to do.

His hands began to shake, and Jack set his jaw in determination. He and his father didn't have enough time left for games or evasions or arguments. Not any more.

Jack opened the door the rest of the way and stepped inside. The sight of his father, frail, swallowed by the hospital bed, took his breath away. He'd aged a lifetime in the six years since he'd seen him last. His skin, gray with illness, stretched tautly over his face; his eyes were sunken and deeply shadowed.

He was propped up in the bed, leaning back against a mountain of pillows, his eyes turned to the corner of the room. Jack followed his gaze. Set up there was his saxophone, just as for years it had been in the corner of the living room.

Jack frowned. The bedroom curtains had been opened wide and sunlight tumbled through. A bird sang in the branch of the tree right outside the window.

But his father would rather gaze into that dark corner. The same as always.

Anger moved through him, and Jack tamped it back. He'd come here to make peace with his father, not more war. "Hello, Dad."

His father turned and looked at him. For a long moment he said nothing, just studied him with an almost hollow indifference. "So, you've come home."

"Yes." His father said nothing, and Jack slipped his hands into his pockets. "To see you."

"Because I'm dying."

"Yes. And because you're my father."

His father coughed, the sound frighteningly raw in the quiet room. "What do you expect me to say to you? Thanks?"

Jack shook his head and took another step closer to the bed. " 'Welcome home,' maybe. Or, that you're glad I'm here."

"Suit yourself." His father turned back to the corner, shutting Jack out.

As he'd always shut him out. For a split second Jack was a child again, hurt, angry. Wishing for his father's attention, his love. The urge to lash out at him rose up in him like a wave, and it took every bit of his maturity and strength of will to fight it back.

He'd ceased being a child long ago. He no longer needed what his father refused to give him. He could make his peace without it. "I'm sorry so much time has passed. I'm sorry our fight has lasted so long. It shouldn't have."

"Save your guilt." His father coughed again, then shuddered, still not looking at him. "I don't need or want it."

The twins pounded up the stairs, then raced down the hall, shrieking and laughing, filling the house with life. With joy.

His father swung to face him. "Shut those kids up, will you? I'm dying, and I still can't get any peace." He sagged against the pillows, weak and exhausted. "Nothing ever changes around here."

Jack thought of his nephews' beaming, beautiful faces, and the anger he'd managed to suppress resurfaced, pushing at the edges of his control. "Is that all you want, Dad? To be alone with your past? With your broken dreams?" Jack jerked his head toward the corner. "To spend the last hours of your life gazing at your shrine?"

His father glowered at him. "Get out. You hear me? I don't want you in here, I don't want any of you in here. I want to be alone."

Jack narrowed his eyes, the pulse pounding in his head. "I didn't come here to get into it with you, but I've had enough. You're one mean, selfish bastard, you know that? You're surrounded by people who care about you, and all you can do is sit here and feel sorry for yourself. It's all you've ever been able to do."

Jack made a sound of derision. "All my life you blamed me and the rest of the family for your unhappiness. You made your own unhappiness. We had nothing to do with it. Don't you think it might be time to grow up and stop blaming others for the choices you made?"

Two spots of bright color tinted his father's cheeks, making him look more alive, healthier than moments before. "I gave up everything for you kids and your mother. I could have been a musician . . . could have had my own ba—"

His words ended on a fit of violent coughing, and for a moment Jack considered letting it go. But there might not be a tomorrow, he thought, and he didn't think he could spend the rest of his life eating the truth. "You didn't give up anything for us, Dad. You chose to give up your music, probably because you were scared you couldn't cut it."

He took a step closer to the bed, his heart pounding. "As for the rest of your life, you threw it away. You threw all of us away. You wasted everything on regret for what you gave up instead of focusing on what you had. You have a beautiful family, a family who stuck by you even though you didn't deserve their love or devotion. You're a lucky man, you always have been."

"So, you're angry at your old man?" His father made a small, weak gesture with his right hand. "You should be thankful instead. Look at yourself. You're a big success, you have everything you ever dreamed of. Ever consider that I might be part of the reason you've done so well? Me and the things I taught you? I helped make you what you are, even if I am a son of a bitch."

Jack stared at his father, stunned. "What?"

"You heard me. I taught you how to live. Me." His father drew a ragged, weak breath. "How far do you think you would have gotten saddled with a family? How far would you have gone if you hadn't wanted to bust out of here so bad? You're my only son, I wasn't about to sit back and let you ruin your life the way I did."

Jack swallowed, suddenly seeing the truth, clearly for the first time. *His father was a bitter and unhappy man not because he had loved—but because he had rejected love.*

Dear God. Jack shook his head, the realization moving over him like a flash fire. He had vowed not to become the man his father was, yet that was exactly what he'd done.

His father had taught him to be like him. To reject love. To be alone.

What had his father just said? That he had everything he'd ever dreamed of. Did he? Was the life he had now, this minute, the one he'd always wanted? Could he look into the future and be contented with the man he was and what he had?

Jack thought of Jill, and his heart turned over. Not by a long shot. Jill was everything he'd ever dreamed of. The way he felt when she looked at him, love shining in her eyes; the way he felt when she was in his arms; the way they held on to each other; the way Rebecca curled her fingers trustingly around his. Those were everything he'd ever dreamed of.

He sucked in a shuddering breath. Jill filled the empty places inside him. She made him happy; she made him whole.

He loved her.

His heart began to thunder against the wall of his chest. Dear Lord, he loved her so much, he thought he might burst with it. He always had.

His father had taught him well, so well that he'd almost thrown away the most wonderful thing in the world, the most important thing.

Love. Jill's love.

He looked at his father, for the first time seeing him as he really was, an unhappy and confused man, a man who had wasted his life on regrets. His anger of moments ago evaporated, replaced by sadness. By pity. His father had had everything, but had refused to see it. Refused to acknowledge it. And now it was too late.

"If my mommy was sick, I'd sit by her bed all night."

Jack smiled, a memory so distant as to be imaginary, coming into his head. Once, his father had sat with him all night. He'd been six and burning with fever. He'd seen monsters that night, beasts of all kinds snapping and snarling at him. His father had stayed with him through it all, reassuring him, promising that the monsters were only visions. When he'd awakened the next morning, his father had still been there.

It may have been Billy Jacobs only instance of fatherly devotion, but it still counted. It was something to hold on to, something wonderful.

Jill.

His heart filled near to bursting with the perfection of loving her. Something wonderful, he thought again. Something to hold on to forever, something real.

He looked at his father's wizened, beaten face, and the anger and fear that had driven him forever evaporated. And was replaced by compassion. By love.

He grabbed the only chair in the room and dragged it over to the bed. He sat down and grinned at his surprised father. "Tell me, Dad, do you still like chocolate ice cream?"

ELEVEN

Jill waited for the judge to arrive, so nervous, she could hardly breathe. She twisted her fingers in her lap, her heart a jackhammer in her chest. Even with the childhood she'd had, these last minutes waiting for the judge were the most lonely and frightening of her life.

She hadn't heard from Jack. She had prayed he would call, had wished and hoped and fantasized that he would change his mind, that he would realize he loved her and that he wanted to be with her forever.

She loved him so much.

She let out a shaky breath. Jack's voice would have calmed her, it would have made her feel less alone. She longed to have someone to cling to for support, someone who loved her.

Not just someone. Jack.

Every part of her life seemed empty without him. She missed him, so much, she ached. She hadn't slept well in the days since she'd watched him walk out of her life. She'd been unable to eat, concentrate, or laugh. She missed laughing the most. She hadn't realized how much she laughed with Jack. She hadn't realized how much she'd smiled, how happy she'd been.

She'd told herself at least a million times that it was for the best, that she'd saved herself and Rebecca from a world of hurt. It had been hard to take comfort in that, however, when she thought she would never be whole again.

Having to face Jack in front of the cameras had been an agony. They'd taped as many shows as possible ahead so that he could go to see his father. The sessions had been less than successful—they'd both been tense, their performances flat. It had hurt so much to look at him that she'd avoiding doing just that, and for the first time they'd had to retape segments of the shows.

She had promised herself she wouldn't let her personal feelings interfere with the job she had to do. She'd tried, really tried, to keep that promise. So had Jack. She'd seen the effort in his expression, heard it in his voice.

Rebecca had been with Peter all week, so she hadn't had her daughter to distract her, to pull her out of herself and into the world of the living. Every night she'd paced the floors of her darkened house, aching for Jack and what would never be, and worrying about the custody hearing and what might be.

It had been all she could do to keep from falling apart.

Peter cleared his throat, and she glanced across the table at him. He looked up and met her eyes. In that moment she thought she saw sympathy in his gaze, and she looked away. Had he known how envious she'd been out in the waiting room as he and Jeanne had clung to each other? Had he seen her longing as they'd leaned on each other, sharing their hopes and fears, their love?

She lowered her eyes to her hands. She'd wished she had the same thing with Jack. She still did.

Dana had been a great friend, supportive and understanding. She had offered to accompany Jill to the hearing, but an emergency at the station had kept her away. Jill tightened her fingers. Maybe it had been for the best. Unlike her and Jack's relationship, Dana and Paul's was going swimmingly. They both glowed with happiness, and although happy for her, Jill couldn't help looking at Dana and seeing what she and Jack had lost.

Jill drew her eyebrows together. *"If you give up now,"* Dana had told her the other day, *"Jack will never love you. If you give up, you may never have a happy ending."*

Jill let Dana's words run through her head, then thought of Jack's as they'd faced each other that final time. *"If you can't have the assurance of perfect love, you're not willing to take a chance. You're afraid, Jill Lansing."*

Was she afraid? Her heart began to thud against the wall of her chest. She drew her eyebrows together again, searching for the truth. Memories of her childhood flooded her mind. Memories of the times she'd reached out to her parents, wanting approval and affection, and been rejected, memories of yearning for love and yet always being without.

Loving Jack scared her to death. Loving him made her feel ten years old again and so vulnerable as to be transparent. She wanted him to love her more than anything. She wanted him to give her everything she'd ever longed for. But she had no guarantees that it would ever happen. She could forever reach out and be rejected. He'd as much as told her so.

But if she didn't try, if she didn't reach out, he would never love her. Never.

Jack had been right, she realized. She began to tremble and clenched her hands tighter in her lap. She'd spent her life running away. Being afraid of not being loved. It's why she'd walked out on him five years before; it's why she'd told him good-bye only days ago.

She was running scared.

No more.

She drew in a deep breath, feeling free for the first time in forever. Feeling whole and vibrant and strong. Love was worth fighting for, she thought, curling her fingers into fists. Jack's love was worth going to war for.

And when this hearing was over, she was going to start doing just that—fighting for Jack's love.

The judge entered the hearing room, his expression solemn. Her lawyer sat beside her, and he reached over and squeezed her hand. "It's going to be all right," he whispered.

She thought of Jack and her resolution, and she stiffened her spine. It would be all right. She was a terrific mother; she provided a wonderful, loving home for Rebecca. And just as Jack had assured her over and over, there was no reason the judge would take her daughter away from her.

A sense of peace moved over her, a momentary calm. She would hold on to that; she would believe everything was going to be all right. And maybe if she believed enough, it would come true.

The judge greeted them, took a seat, and began the proceedings.

Peter was questioned first, and his lawyer started by questioning him about his relationship with Rebecca.

Peter answered, his voice clear and without tremor. Jill breathed deeply through her nose. She'd wasted her time worrying about what he might say about her past or present relationship with Jack; it didn't come up. Neither did her association with *Reel Reviews*.

He came off as a level-headed and devoted father who loved his daughter very much.

Her lawyer took over then. He smiled at Peter. "You're an accountant, Mr. Knight. Is that right?"

"Yes, that's correct. I own my own firm."

"You're doing well." Her lawyer leaned back in his chair, the picture of casual interest. "It must be quite demanding, owning your own firm. Long hours, a lot of headaches."

Peter smiled. "It is. But I enjoy it."

The lawyer picked up his pen and ran it back and forth through his fingers. "Tax time must be crazy. Everybody waits until the last minute, everybody wants an extension. I know my accountant works around the clock."

"That's about it." Peter shrugged. "But I'm used to it."

"Those kinds of demands must keep you away from home a lot."

Peter's smile slipped. "They do. But Jeanne's there." He looked at Jill. "She doesn't work outside the home, and she's a very good mother."

Peter's barb struck home, and Jill cringed, but her lawyer went on, unperturbed.

"So you're saying that Jeanne's there to take care of the children's needs when you have to work late?"

"Yes. And she's great with Rebecca. She loves her very much."

"I'm sure." The lawyer lowered his eyes to his pen, then looked at Peter once more. "How many nights, on the average, are you late coming home from the office?"

Peter stiffened. "Two or three."

"That's during tax time?"

Peter hesitated. "No, during tax time it's pretty . . . constant."

"I see. So, you're saying that if you get custody of Rebecca, she'll be cared for totally by Jeanne two or three times a week, minimum?"

"Yes. But Jeanne is a terrific—"

"I'm sure she is. Thank you, Mr. Knight."

Then it was Jill's turn. "Ms. Lansing, why don't you tell me about your relationship with your daughter," her lawyer began.

Jill folded her trembling hands in front of her. She met the judge's gaze evenly. "What would you like to know? There are so many aspects to our relationship."

"Why don't you tell me what makes your relationship special?"

Jill dropped her hands to her lap, thinking of her daughter and the time they spent together. An involuntary smile touched her mouth. "I'm her mother. I've spent more time with her than anybody else has. I was the first person to hold her, I nursed her in the middle of the night, rocked her when she was sick."

She breathed deeply, letting the oxygen steady her. "I look at her and feel such love, such pride." She met the judge's eyes once more. "When I look at her, I feel so much, my heart hardly feels big enough to hold it all."

She clasped her hands tighter in her lap, willing her voice to stop quivering, wishing she could sound as calm and in control as Peter had. "There's a bond between us, a special kind of communication. I know what she needs, how she feels, even before she does. I don't know how else to explain it. She doesn't have it with anyone else, even Peter who I know she loves very much."

The judge was silent as he made notes. Her lawyer continued. "Ms. Lansing what are your plans for Rebecca? Your hopes and dreams? And how do you plan to help her achieve them?"

"My biggest hope for her is that she be happy. I want her to grow into a secure, self-confident adult. I want her to know how wonderful she is and that she's loved." Emotion welled up inside her, choking her, and she cleared her throat. "I'll nurture those feeling by letting her make choices, by offering her a wealth of opportunities, and by always believing in her."

The judge smiled at her, just a slight curving of his lips, and her hopes soared. She had spoken from her heart and it had made a difference.

Peter's lawyer questioned her extensively about her job and the number of hours she worked, even bringing up *Reel Reviews* and the publicity campaign she'd participated in. She sailed confidently through them, still buoyed by the judge's small smile.

The judge called the witnesses, hers first. Both Margaret and Julie, Rebecca's teacher, said what a good mother she was, how much Rebecca loved her and how close the two were.

Jill smiled at the women in thanks, feeling really good about their testimony until Jeanne came in and started to talk. With a sinking heart Jill listened as Jeanne gushed over Peter's relationship with Rebecca, describing in loving detail what a good father he was.

She described how Rebecca ran to him when he came home from work, how he would swing his daughter high into the air, then carry her on his shoulders to the kitchen to greet the rest of the family.

Her witnesses had made her sound like a great mother; Jeanne made him sound like a dream father. He sounded like a father who should be sainted. She had gotten a smile from the judge; Jeanne got a beam that could light up the Statue of Liberty.

Heart sinking, Jill watched the judge's expression change as Jeanne spoke. It softened, warmed. Some of the earlier sternness evaporated.

The bitter taste of fear filled her mouth; her head began to throb; her palms and armpits to sweat. She couldn't lose Rebecca. She couldn't.

As if sensing her rising panic, her lawyer reached across and squeezed her clenched hands reassuringly, then turned his attention to Peter's wife.

"Mrs. Knight," he began, "you've talked a great deal about Peter's relationship with Rebecca, but little about yours. What kind of relationship do you have with your husband's daughter?"

"What do you mean?"

He lifted his shoulders. "Do you love her?"

"Oh, yes." Jeanne looked at Peter, then back at the lawyer. "She's a very sweet child. And very important to Peter. I've been helping care for her since she was two."

"So you know her well?"

"Oh, yes."

"I understand you and your husband have another child."

Jeanne smiled proudly. "She's eight months now."

"Congratulations. You must be thrilled."

"Ecstatic."

"And you'll have no problem caring for two young children."

"No." She shook her head. "I do it already."

"Part-time," he corrected. "After all, Rebecca's only there two weeks a month."

He picked up his pen and began turning it in his fingers. Jill watched him, her pulse drumming. He'd done the exact same thing while questioning Peter—the moment before he'd gone straight for the jugular.

"Do you enjoy having Rebecca with you?" he asked softly.

She frowned as if confused. "Yes, very much."

"Of course." The pen stilled. "But surely there are times when she's with you when you wish it was just the three of you . . . you, your child, and your husband."

Jeanne hesitated, two bright spots of coloring tinting her cheeks. She looked at Peter as if for guidance, and Jill saw him nod slightly as if telling her to go on.

"Well," she said, "I don't think it would be natural if I didn't wish that once in a while. And I don't think it would be honest of me to deny it."

He tossed down the pen. "Do you have a picture of your baby, Mrs. Knight?"

"Of course."

He smiled. "I'd love to see a picture of her. May I?" He rose and crossed to Jeanne's seat.

She reached for her purse, took out her wallet, and flipped it open. "Those are both of her." She indicated the photo on the right. "There she's six months. In the other she's six days."

He studied the photos a moment. "She's adorable."

He handed the wallet back. "Do you have a picture of Rebecca?"

Jeanne flushed and with shaking hands took the wallet from him. "Well . . . no. Peter has several, though. And that doesn't mean I don't care for Rebecca," she added, her voice rising. "Because I do. Very much. I told you that."

"I believe you do, Mrs. Knight. Absolutely. I've met Rebecca, and it would take a pretty heartless person not to like her. But do you love her?" Jeanne opened her mouth to answer, and he added, "Do you love her as much as your baby?"

Jeanne's eyes flooded with tears. For a moment she said nothing, and Jill could see how she struggled to hold the tears back, how she struggled for control. Even though Jill felt like cheering, she felt sympathy for the other woman as well.

She looked at her husband, her glance beseeching, then down at her folded hands. "No," she whispered. "I do love her, but . . . how could I love her as much as my own? I carried her, I gave birth to her, I . . ."

Her voice trailed helplessly off. Heart pounding with hope, Jill looked from Jeanne to the judge to her exhusband. Peter looked stunned, the judge solemn. She said a silent prayer of thanks.

"Thank you, Mrs. Knight," her lawyer said softly. "You were most helpful."

The judge cleared his throat and stood. "I've heard enough to make my decision, though I will need a few moments to sort out my thoughts and look over my notes."

"Your Honor?" Peter got to his feet. "Would it be

possible for my wife to be with me while you announce your decision?"

The judge nodded and looked at Jill. "If there's anyone you wish to have with you, feel free to call them in."

A lump in her throat, she thanked him. She lowered her eyes to her hands, thinking of Jack, wishing she could walk out to the waiting room and into his arms. Wishing he were there with her, no matter the terms.

Love was worth fighting for. Jack's love was worth going to war for.

"I need some air," she whispered to her lawyer, standing and, with trembling fingers, smoothing her skirt. "I'll be right outside."

He nodded and she crossed to the door and stepped out into the cool hallway. She shut her eyes and took a deep, steadying breath. Just a little longer, she told herself. In just a little while—

"Jilly!"

She opened her eyes and swung around, her heart beginning to thrum against the wall of her chest. Jack stood at the other end of the hallway, a garment bag slung over his shoulder. As she met his gaze, he started toward her, striding, then jogging, down the crowded hallway.

She brought a hand to her throat, joy blooming inside her. He'd come to be with her, even after their confrontation. Because he'd known how much she needed him. And because maybe, just maybe, he needed her too.

He reached her and slid the bag from his shoulder, letting it drop to the floor. "Jilly," he said, catching her hands, closing his protectively around them.

She searched his face, drinking in the sight of him.

He looked like he hadn't slept in days, like he'd been through the tortures of hell and back. Yet she saw something in his eyes she never had before. Something warm, intimate. Something that made her heart turn over.

"I came straight from the airport." He caught his breath. "What's happened? Is it over?" When she didn't respond, he clasped her hands tighter, his expression frantic with worry. "Has the judge made his decision?"

She opened her mouth, but nothing came out. Happiness had stolen her ability to speak, to think, to do anything but feel. Tears filled her eyes, this time ones of pure joy.

Jack murmured a soft oath and drew her against his chest, holding her tightly. "You can lean on me, sweetheart. I'm here for you, I promise."

He trailed his fingers through her hair; against her cheek she could feel the runaway beat of his heart. "I missed you so much," he murmured. "It's been hell. I couldn't stop thinking about you and about Rebecca I couldn't stop worrying."

She tipped her head back and met his eyes, almost afraid to know why he'd come today, afraid to hope he'd come because of something more than concern. "Jack, I—" Her throat closed over the words, and she fought to clear it. "I need to know . . . I—"

"Jill, the judge has made his decision."

She looked over her shoulder at her lawyer, and an involuntary shudder of fear moved over her. Jack caught her hand and twined his fingers with hers.

"It's going to be okay," he murmured. "We've got to believe that."

We, she thought, gripping his hand. Did that mean what she hoped it did? Did that mean they were a team now? That they were in this together, they had each other to lean on and to support?

"Thank you for being here," she whispered, realizing that no matter the outcome of their love affair, no matter the reason he had come, it meant more than anything to her that he had.

Without another word they walked into the hearing room and took their places at the table, hands still clasped. She tightened her fingers on his, taking the strength he offered, finding comfort in the feel of his hand around hers.

The judge began to speak. "I want you both to know this was an extremely difficult decision for me to make. Rebecca's a lucky little girl. You both love your daughter very much, you're both determined to give her a good home and a wonderful life." He drew a thoughtful breath. "It came down to me having to make a choice I did not relish making."

He folded his hands in front of him. "I asked myself which home would be better for Rebecca. Which parent could provide the most stable and nurturing environment."

The judge looked at her ex-husband; and a small sound of fear raced to her lips. Jack tightened his fingers.

"I've decided to award custody to Rebecca's mother."

For a split second she couldn't breathe, couldn't focus on a thought, couldn't feel anything but a numbing relief. *She hadn't lost Rebecca. Thank God . . . Thank God.*

Even as the judge went on to explain why he'd awarded her custody, the numbness retreated, leaving joy in its place. When he'd finished, she turned to Jack, feeling as if she might burst with happiness. "It's over," she said, throwing her arms around him. "I'm not going to lose her."

Jack hugged her back. "I'm so happy, Jilly. So happy."

The next minutes passed in a blur. She thanked her lawyer and spoke to the judge. She turned to look for Peter and found him gazing at her, his expression twisted with grief. Sympathy moved through her—she understood what he must be feeling right now, how much he must hurt.

She crossed to where he stood, stopping before him. "I'm sorry, Peter." She touched his arm. "I'm sorry one of us had to lose."

He looked away, then back. "The one who really loses is Rebecca."

Jill couldn't deny that, although she wished she could. Rebecca loved her father and it would hurt her to see him only every other weekend. The next months would be difficult for their daughter; she would no doubt be sad and confused, no matter how patiently and lovingly they explained the situation to her.

"She'll never be farther than a phone call away," Jill said. "Whenever you want to see her, just call."

His eyes grew bright with emotion, and he stiffened, fighting it. "I wanted to tell you that I was sorry. I didn't know Jeanne felt that way about Rebecca. I didn't think . . ." He curled his hands into fists. "All I thought about was how much I loved my daughter, and how much I would miss her if you got custody."

Sympathy moved through her. It had taken much for her ex-husband to say those words; he was a proud and stubborn man. "You'll never lose her, Peter. You'll always be her father, and she'll always love you."

His mouth twisted with bitter disappointment. "That's easy for you to say now, isn't it? I bet you wouldn't feel that way if you were in my shoes."

"No, you're right. I wouldn't." She touched his sleeve. "But I am sorry."

He opened his mouth as if to say something more, then shut it. He shook his head. "Jeanne's waiting. I'll be talking to you soon."

Jill watched him walk away, emotion choking her. This had been a no-win situation from the beginning, and she couldn't help feeling a measure of responsibility for it.

Jack came up behind her. "What are you thinking?" he asked softly, placing his hands on her shoulders.

She looked up at him. They were alone in the hearing room, and save for the noise from the hallway, the room was quiet. "About Peter. About the past."

"I thought so. You looked so sad."

She turned and placed her hands on his chest. "I'm not sad. I'm happy. Deliriously happy." She searched his gaze. "It's over. Finally."

"No." He cupped her face, his expression so tender, it took her breath. "It's just beginning. Finally."

Hope flourished inside her. "What do you mean, Jack?"

He leaned closer. "I mean that from this day forward, I'll be there for you. Emotionally and in every other way. It means that I realized what a fool I've been, that I've been throwing away my life, my one chance at real happiness."

He smiled softly. "You're that chance. You always

have been. I love you, Jill Lansing. I want to spend today with you, and tomorrow. I want to spend forever with you."

Wonder and joy filled her. She curved her arms around him, holding him tightly. Forever, she thought. They would be together forever, and even that wouldn't be enough time in his arms. She tipped her head back and met his gaze. "Jack, what happened? Last time we talked, you said you would never love—"

"Don't," Jack interrupted softly, placing his fingers against her mouth. "I never want to hear those words again. I could have lost you."

He moved his fingers almost reverently over her face, and she had the sense that he needed to reassure himself that she was in his arms, that she was real.

"I saw my dad," he murmured. "He's so sick. It hurt to see him that way. It hurt badly."

"I'm sorry, Jack." She cupped his face tenderly. "So sorry."

He tipped his face into her caress. "I finally understand him. I finally see him for who he is—a lonely man who pushed everyone who cared about him away, a man who lived without ever knowing the joy of loving.

"He had everything, but he refused to see it. He refused to accept the wonderful thing that was being given to him." Jack hesitated. "I looked at him and saw myself."

"No." Jill shook her head. "You're not like him, Jack. You're not."

"Not anymore, but I was becoming like him. I—" His throat closed over the words, and he cleared it. "I almost lost you, Jilly. I almost closed myself off to love.

The love you offered me, the love I feel for you. Rebecca's love."

He bent his head close to hers. "I love you, Jilly. And it feels so wonderful. I never want to be without your love again."

"You never will be," she murmured thickly. "I love you, Jack. Forever."

Smiling with a happiness he couldn't even have imagined before, he brought her mouth to his.

THE EDITOR'S CORNER

Prepare to be swept off your feet by the four sizzling LOVESWEPT romances available next month. Never mind puppy love—you're soon to experience the tumultuous effects of desperation and passion in this spring's roller-coaster of romance.

Bestselling author Fayrene Preston turns up the heat with **LADY BEWARE,** LOVESWEPT #742. Kendall Merrick trusts Steven Gant when she should be running for her life. From the moment they meet, she is certain she knows him—knows his warmth, his scent, and the heat of his caress—but it just isn't possible! Steven hints she is in danger, then tempts her with fiery kisses that make her forget any fear. Has she surrendered to a stranger who will steal her soul? Find out in this spellbinding tale from Fayrene Preston.

Change gears with Marcia Evanick's playful but passionate **EMMA AND THE HAND-SOME DEVIL,** LOVESWEPT #743. She figures Brent Haywood will be happy to sell his half of Amazing Grace, but when the gorgeous hunk says he is staying, Emma Carson wonders what he could possibly want with a chicken farm—or her! Fascinated by his spunky housemate, Brent senses her yearnings, guesses at the silk she wears beneath the denim, and hopes that his lips can silence her fear of never being enough for him. Discover if opposites really do attract as Marcia Evanick explores the humor and touching emotion of unexpected love.

THICK AS THIEVES, LOVESWEPT #744, is Janis Reams Hudson's latest steamy suspense. Undercover agent Harper Montgomery stands alone as his brother is buried, remembering how Mike had stolen his future and married the woman who should have been *his* wife. Now, ten years later, Annie is no longer the carefree woman he remembers. Harper is determined to learn the bitter truth behind the sadness and fear in her eyes—and find out whether there is anything left of the old Annie, the one who had sworn their love was forever. Janis Reams Hudson fans the flames of reawakened love in this sizzling contemporary romance.

Join us in welcoming new author Riley Morse as we feature her sparkling debut, **INTO THE STORM,** LOVESWEPT #745. If all is fair in love and war, Dr. Ryan Jericho declares the battle lines drawn! Summer Keaton's golden beauty is true temptation, but the software she has designed will cost him a halfway house for kids he counsels—unless he distracts her long enough to break the deal. Scorched by a gaze that lights a fire of longing, Summer struggles to survive his seduction strategy without losing her heart. Riley Morse creates a pair of tantalizing adversaries in this fabulous love story.

Happy reading,

With warmest wishes!

Beth de Guzman   Shauna Summers

Senior Editor   Associate Editor

P.S. Don't miss the exciting women's fiction Bantam has coming in June: In **FAIREST OF THEM ALL,** Teresa Medeiros's blockbuster medieval romance, Sir Austyn of Gavenmore, in search of a plain bride, wins Holly de Chastel in a tournament, never suspecting her to be the fairest woman in all of England; Geralyn Dawson's enticing new charmer, **TEMPTING MO-RALITY**, has Zach Burnett conceiving a plan to use Morality Brown for his personal revenge—only to have the miracle of love save his soul. Look for a sneak peek at these dazzling books in next month's LOVESWEPT. And immediately following this page, look for a preview of the terrific romances from Bantam that are *available now!*

Don't miss these extraordinary books
by your favorite Bantam authors

On sale in April:

DARK RIDER
by Iris Johansen

LOVE STORM
by Susan Johnson

PROMISE ME MAGIC
by Patricia Camden

"Iris Johansen is one of the romance genre's finest treasures."
—*Romantic Times*

DARK RIDER

by the *New York Times* bestselling author

IRIS JOHANSEN

New York Times *bestselling author Iris Johansen is a "master among master storytellers"* and her bestselling novels have won every major romance award, including the coveted* Romantic Times *Lifetime Achievement Award. Now discover the spellbinding world of Iris Johansen in her most tantalizing novel yet.*

From the moment she heard of the arrival of the English ship, Cassandra Deville sensed danger. But she never expected the sensuous invader who stepped out of the shadows of the palms and onto the moonlit beach. Bold, passionate, electrifyingly masculine, Jared Danemount made it clear he had every intention of destroying her father. But he hardly knew what to make of the exquisite, pagan creature who offered herself to him, defiantly declaring that she

* Affaire de Coeur

*would use his desire to her own advantage. Still, he could
no more resist her challenge than he could ignore the temptation to risk everything for the heart of a woman sworn to
betray him.*

"Are you truly a virgin?"

She stiffened and then whirled to face the man
strolling out of the thatch of palms. He spoke in the
Polynesian language she had used with her friends,
but there could be no doubt that he was not one of
them. He was as tall but leaner and moved with a
slow, casual grace, not with the springy exuberance of
the islanders. He was dressed in elegant tight
breeches and his coat fit sleekly over his broad shoulders. His snowy cravat was tied in a complicated fall
and his dark hair bound back in a queue.

*He is very beautiful and has the grace and lusty appe-
tite of that stallion you love so much.*

Her friend Lihua had said those words and she
was right. He *was* beautiful. Exotic grace and strength
exuded from every limb. High cheekbones and that
well-formed, sensual mouth gave his face a fascinating
quality that made it hard to tear her gaze away. A
stray breeze ruffled his dark hair and a lock fell across
his wide forehead.

Pagan.

The word came out of nowhere and she instantly
dismissed it. Their housekeeper Clara used the term
to describe the islanders and she would deem it totally
unfit for civilized young noblemen. Yet there
was something free and reckless flickering in the
stranger's expression that she had never seen in any of
the islanders.

Yes, he must be the Englishman; he was coming from the direction of King Kamehameha's village, she realized. He probably only wanted supplies or trade rights as the other English did. She did not have to worry about him.

"Well, are you?" he asked lazily as he continued to walk toward her.

He might not be a threat but she answered with instinctive wariness. "You should not eavesdrop on others' conversations. It's not honorable."

"I could hardly keep from hearing. You were shouting." His gaze wandered from her face to her bare breasts and down to her hips swathed in the cotton sarong. "And I found the subject matter so very intriguing. It was exceptionally . . . arousing. It's not every day a man is compared to a stallion."

His arrogance and confidence were annoying. "Lihua is easily pleased."

He looked startled, but then a slow smile lit his face. "And you are not, if you're still a virgin. What a challenge to a man. What is your name?"

"What is yours?"

"Jared."

"You have another name."

His brows lifted. "You're not being fair. You've not told me your name yet." He bowed. "But, if we must be formal, I'm Jared Barton Danemount."

"And you're a duke?"

"I have that honor . . . or dishonor. Depending upon my current state of dissipation. Does that impress you?"

"No, it's only another word for chief, and we have many chiefs here."

He laughed. "I'm crushed. Now that we've established my relative unimportance, may I ask your name?"

"Kanoa." It was not a lie. It was the Polynesian name she had been given, and meant more to her than her birth name.

"The free one," the Englishman translated. "But you're not free. Not if this person you called the ugly one keeps you from pleasure."

"That's none of your concern."

"On the contrary, I hope to make it very much my concern. I've had very good news tonight and I feel like celebrating. Will you celebrate with me, Kanoa?"

His smile shimmered in the darkness, coaxing, alluring. Nonsense. He was only a man; it was stupid to be so fascinated by this stranger. "Why should I? Your good news is nothing to me."

"Because it's a fine night and I'm a man and you're a woman. Isn't that enough?"

LOVE STORM
by Susan Johnson

"Susan Johnson is one of the best."
—*Romantic Times*

*Desperate to avoid a loathsome match, Zena Turku ran
from the glittering ballroom in the snowy night and threw
herself at the mercy of a darkly handsome stranger. He was
her only hope of escape, her one guarantee of safe passage to
her ancestral home in the Caucasus mountains. But Prince
Alexander Kuzan mistook the alluring redhead for a lady
of the evening, the perfect plaything to relieve the boredom
of his country journey. Only after her exquisite innocence
was revealed did the most notorious rake of St. Petersburg
realize that his delicious game of seduction had turned into
a conquest of his heart.*

Zena experienced a frightening feeling of vulnerability when this darkly handsome prince touched her;
it was as though she no longer belonged to herself, as
though he controlled her passion with his merest
touch.

The prince must think her the most degraded
wanton to allow him such liberties, to actually beg for
release in his arms. A deep sense of humiliation swept
over her as she tried to reconcile this astonishing, un-
precedented sensuousness with the acceptable behavior required of young society debutantes. How could

she have permitted these rapturous feelings of hers to overcome her genteel upbringing? Certainly the prince would never respect her now.

Zena's eyelashes fluttered up and she gazed surreptitiously from under their shield at the man who had so casually taken her virginity. He was disturbingly handsome: fine, aristocratic features; full, sensitive mouth; dark, long, wavy hair; smooth bronze skin. The brilliance of a huge emerald caught her eye as his hand rested possessively on her hip, making her acutely aware of the contrast between their circumstances. He was handsome, rich, charming, seductively expert, she ruefully noted. Plainly she had made a fool of herself, and her mortification was absolute. But then she reminded herself sharply that *anything* was superior to having to wed that odious toad of a general, and the prince *was* taking her away from St. Petersburg.

The emerald twinkled in the subdued light as Alex gently brushed the damp curls from Zena's cheek. "I'm sorry for hurting you, *ma petite*," he whispered softly. "I had no idea this was your first evening as a streetwalker. Had I known, I could have been more gentle."

At which point Prince Alexander was presented with some fascinating information, most of which he would have quite willingly remained in ignorance of.

"I'm not a streetwalker, my lord."

Alex's black brows snapped together in a sudden scowl. *Bloody hell, what have I got into?*

"I'm the daughter of Baron Turku from Astrakhan."

The scowl deepened noticeably.

"My father died six months ago, and my aunt began trying to marry me off to General Scobloff."

The frown lifted instantly, and Alex breathed a sigh of relief. At least, he mentally noted, there were no irate relatives to reckon with immediately. "Sweet Jesus! That old vulture must be close to seventy!" he exclaimed, horrified.

"Sixty-one, my lord, and he's managed to bury two wives already," Zena quietly murmured. "I didn't want to become his wife, but my aunt was insisting, so I simply had to get away. My little brother and I will—"

"Little brother?" Alex sputtered. "The young child isn't yours?" he asked in confusion, and then remembered. Of course he wasn't hers; Alex had just taken her virginity! A distinct feeling of apprehension and, on the whole, disagreeable sensations struck the young prince. *Merde!* This just wasn't his night! "You deliberately led me on," he accused uncharitably, choosing to ignore the fact that he had drunk so much in the past fifteen hours that his clarity of thought was not at peak performance.

"I did not lead you on!" Zena returned tartly, angry that the prince should think she had contrived this entire situation. "Modest young ladies of good breeding do not lead men on!" she snapped.

"Permit me to disagree, my pet, for I've known many modest young ladies of good breeding," Alex disputed coolly, "a number of whom have led me on to the same, ah, satisfactory conclusion we have just enjoyed. They're all quite willing once the tiresome conventional posturing has been observed."

The prince's obvious competence in an area of

connoisseurship completely foreign to Zena's limited sphere served to squelch her ingenuous assertion.

Alex sighed disgruntledly. *Good God, for which of my sins am I paying penance?* "What am I to do with you—a damnable virgin? Of all the rotten luck! You try to be helpful and come to the aid of what appears to be a nice, ordinary streetwalker and look what happens. She turns out to be a cursed green virgin with a baby brother to boot, not to mention a respectable family."

"No, my lord, no family," Zena quietly reminded him.

A faintly pleased glint of relief momentarily shone in the depths of the golden eyes. "Thank God for small favors. Nevertheless, you, my dear, have become a vexatious problem," Alex censoriously intoned.

"You could take the honorable course of action and marry me, my lord."

PROMISE ME MAGIC

by the extraordinarily talented

Patricia Camden

"A strong new voice in historical fiction . . . This is an author to watch!"
—*Romantic Times*

With a fury born of fear, Katharina had taken aim at the bandit who dared to trespass on her land and fired only to discover that the powerful warrior she felled was a man she thought long dead . . . a man who had stolen her fortune . . . a man she despised. Now, as she gazed into Alexandre von Löwe's smoldering gray eyes and felt the overpowering pull of his attraction, she wondered why she'd let the scoundrel live and how she was going to tell him she was masquerading as his wife. . . .

"I am Katharina von Melle," she told him, then waited as if expecting a response.

"Madame von Melle," he said, giving her a slight nod. He grimaced and bit back a ripe oath. Someone had just lit the powder touchhole of the cannon in his head.

"Katharina," the woman gritted out as if to a slow wit. "Anna. Magdalena. von Melle."

Obviously, she thought he should know her. A

memory niggled, but it was beyond grasping in his fuzzy head. Christ, she was beautiful. Full lips hinting at a sensual nature that belied the coldness in her eyes, the bones—if not her manner or her clothes—telling of well-bred nobility.

A former lover? Had he passed the long months of a year's winter quarters spending his passion in that glorious voluptuous body? One forgot a great many things in war, some by accident, others for the sake of sanity, but, sweet God, he'd take her gun and shoot himself if he could ever have forgotten that body—or those eyes.

Katharina von Melle. It felt as if he should remember it, but . . . nothing. "Madame von Melle, of course!" he prevaricated. "The wounds of war have addled my wits. Such eyes as those would be forever burned into any man's memor—" The slender finger curling on the trigger tightened. "I mean, that is—"

" 'I mean, that is' . . . utter nonsense, Colonel von Löwe," she said, her gaze as steady as a cat's. "If there is any burning to be done, it will be into your body by a lead ball."

As a cat's . . . Katharina von Melle. *Oh, Jesus.* "Kat," he said. "You're Father's Kat." They had never met, but he knew her. God save him, he knew her.

"You blanch quite nicely," she told him. "I take it you recognize the name? Your *ward*, my dear Colonel. I was your ward. First your father's, then *yours*. Do you remember now? I was part of your inheritance, remember? Your eldest brother was to get the north end of this valley, complete with the lucrative mill, your middle brother was to get all the land in the middle, from the peak known as the Mule in the west to the Carabas River. And you—all you were to inherit was the small manor house of Löwe and a mangy spinster named Kat. And you did inherit. First the house and me, and then the rest of it when your brothers died, and all without bothering to leave your precious war."

He wanted to sleep and the careless irritation that comes from being deprived of it was gnawing at his sense of preservation. "Did you truly expect me to leave my regiment and come home to a ramshackle old house to nursemaid the bastard daughter of some friend of my father's I don't even know? The French had entered the war! Old alliances were falling apart; new alliances were being formed. It was as if a puddle of mercury had dispersed into a hundred bubbles, some that would save you, others that would prove fatal." He shrugged, but had to look away from the winter in her eyes. "An ink-stained lawyer's clerk sent word that you were living with friends in the Tausend capital. It seemed adequate to me. I had more important things to deal with—such as a war."

"War or no, alliances or no—you still managed to turn inheriting this Kat into a profit, didn't you? A ten-thousand thaler profit! My marriage portion. But I didn't know that then, did I? No. I discovered it six years ago when word came that you were dead. At last! At age twenty-two I found myself mistress of my fortune and my fate—except, of course, that there was no fortune. That loss cost me dearly, von Löwe. But though you cost me while alive, by being dead you have managed to partially pay me back. Löwe Manor is mine."

"Impossible."

"No, Colonel von Löwe, *possible*. In fact, more than possible. It has been done. A fait accompli. Löwe Manor is mine. For four years I have lived there, and no one has challenged me." A mixture of guilt and bravado flashed through her eyes, the same look a woman gets who has cheated on her lover and now seeks to deny it. He had barely registered that it was there before it was gone. She sighted again down the barrel of the pistol with renewed determination.

"And now, Colonel, though you neglected to give me a choice about my future when you stole my fortune from me, I shall give you a choice about yours. You can choose to leave—with Löwe remaining in my possession—or you can choose to contest my ownership. Of course, if you choose the latter, the hero dies, shot for a brigand on his way home. Such a shame."

"So the bastard daughter would turn murderer? Such a shame."

He heard her lick her lips. "You and Tragen and the other one can move to Alte Veste. It is but a day's ride from here."

"A day's ride straight up. It's coming on to winter, Kat . . . Katharina," he said carefully. "Alte Veste is deserted, and has been for three generations. Cold, too, and full of drafts. Tragen would probably succumb."

He waited, his breathing nearly suspended. He needed the obscurity that Löwe Manor could provide —at least until late February or early March. And after that, given von Mecklen's delight in all things ravaged, they all would most likely be looking for a new place to live. If they were still alive.

"You may stay until Tragen has recovered enough to travel. But you must give me your word that Löwe is mine."

He sucked in a breath of victory. "You have it."

"Say the words."

"I give you my word that Löwe Manor will be yours."

"Not will be . . . *is!*" She moved around to where Alexandre could see her, and what he saw made him go still inside. Distrust, despair, and an iron will to go on. It was the look of a woman touched too closely by war. He'd seen it before, on other women's faces, on those who had survived.

"Löwe is yours," he said softly.

"And . . . and you must accept whatever you find there."

He narrowed his eyes. "Why? What will I find there?" She did not answer. "What will I find there, Kat?" Silence. He let his head fall back to the folded wool, but through his lashes he could still see the black point of the pistol barrel aimed at him. "I will accept whatever I find there . . . within the restrictions of my oaths to the emperor, the duke of Tausend, and my men."

The gun barrel did not waver for a heartbeat. Then two . . . three . . .

"Cross me and you're a dead man," Katharina said with the tempered steel of conviction. And lowered the pistol.

He closed his eyes in relief. Whatever desperate hold he'd had on his awareness left him then, and he began to slip into sleep.

A nudge roused him to semiawareness. "Colonel

von Löwe," she called, nudging him again. "Colonel, there's one thing you should know before we reach Löwe Manor."

He grunted, drifting back into oblivion.

"I'm your wife."

Alexandre woke up.

And don't miss these electrifying
romances from Bantam Books,
on sale in May:

FAIREST OF THEM ALL
by bestselling author
Teresa Medeiros
"Teresa Medeiros writes rare love
stories to cherish."
—*Romantic Times*

TEMPTING MORALITY
by award-winning author
Geralyn Dawson
"[Geralyn Dawson] weaves a deliciously
arousing tale."
—*Affaire de Coeur*

OFFICIAL RULES NO PURCHASE NECESSARY

To enter the sweepstakes outlined below, you must respond by the date specified and follow all entry instructions published elsewhere in this offer.

DREAM COME TRUE SWEEPSTAKES

Sweepstakes begins 9/1/94, ends 1/15/96. To qualify for the Early Bird Prize, entry must be received by the date specified elsewhere in this offer. Winners will be selected in random drawings on 2/29/96 by an independent judging organization whose decisions are final. Early Bird winner will be selected in a separate drawing from among all qualifying entries.

Odds of winning determined by total number of entries received. Distribution not to exceed 300 million.

Estimated maximum retail value of prizes: Grand (1) $25,000 (cash alternative $20,000); First (1) $2,000; Second (1) $750; Third (50) $75; Fourth (1,000) $50; Early Bird (1) $5,000. Total prize value: $86,500.

Automobile and travel trailer must be picked up at a local dealer; all other merchandise prizes will be shipped to winners. Awarding of any prize to a minor will require written permission of parent/guardian. If a trip prize is won by a minor, s/he must be accompanied by parent/legal guardian. Trip prizes subject to availability and must be completed within 12 months of date awarded. Blackout dates may apply. Early Bird trip is on a space available basis and does not include port charges, gratuities, optional shore excursions and onboard personal purchases. Prizes are not transferable or redeemable for cash except as specified. No substitution for prizes except as necessary due to unavailability. Travel trailer and/or automobile license and registration fees are winners' responsibility as are any other incidental expenses not specified herein.

Early Bird Prize may not be offered in some presentations of this sweepstakes. Grand through third prize winners will have the option of selecting any prize offered at level won. All prizes will be awarded. Drawing will be held at 204 Center Square Road, Bridgeport, NJ 08014. Winners need not be present. For winners list (available in June, 1996), send a self-addressed, stamped envelope by 1/15/96 to: Dream Come True Winners, P.O. Box 572, Gibbstown, NJ 08027.

THE FOLLOWING APPLIES TO THE SWEEPSTAKES ABOVE:

No purchase necessary. No photocopied or mechanically reproduced entries will be accepted. Not responsible for lost, late, misdirected, damaged, incomplete, illegible, or postage-die mail. Entries become the property of sponsors and will not be returned.

Winner(s) will be notified by mail. Winner(s) may be required to sign and return an affidavit of eligibility/release within 14 days of date on notification or an alternate may be selected. Except where prohibited by law entry constitutes permission to use of winners' names, hometowns, and likenesses for publicity without additional compensation. Void where prohibited or restricted. All federal, state, provincial, and local laws and regulations apply.

All prize values are in U.S. currency. Presentation of prizes may vary; values at a given prize level will be approximately the same. All taxes are winners' responsibility.

Canadian residents, in order to win, must first correctly answer a time-limited skill testing question administered by mail. Any litigation regarding the conduct and awarding of a prize in this publicity contest by a resident of the province of Quebec may be submitted to the Regie des loteries et courses du Quebec.

Sweepstakes is open to legal residents of the U.S., Canada, and Europe (in those areas where made available) who have received this offer.

Sweepstakes in sponsored by Ventura Associates, 1211 Avenue of the Americas, New York, NY 10036 and presented by independent businesses. Employees of these, their advertising agencies and promotional companies involved in this promotion, and their immediate families, agents, successors, and assignees shall be ineligible to participate in the promotion and shall not be eligible for any prizes covered herein. SWP 3/95